Shadow over our Valley

Ian J Currie

Shadow over our Valley

Preface

Shadow over our Valley is a story of a coalmine disaster above the village of Pentrebach, somewhere in a South Wales valley. The disaster occurred due to a firedamp gas explosion, the result of which trapped twenty-one men and four young boys in a limited space where the water level was rising with its inevitable consequences.

Due to the quantity and solidity of the resulting rock fall, the miners were unable to dig themselves free and for the same reason the would-be rescuers unable to reach them.

This failure to bring about the miners liberty or even recover a single body, placed a heavy burden upon the villagers of Pentrebach and over time became synonymous with not only the village but the entire valley of Aber-Afon-Gwen.

The irony of this incident is that it took place in 1863, just two years before legislation obligating mine owners to incorporate both an ingress and egress in all coalmines was introduced under an Act of Parliament;

had this been in being at the time an alternative escape route might well have saved the twenty-five victims of Pentrebach.

Add to this the case that a number of coalmine owners in the Welsh valleys had voluntarily introduced two outlets into their works prior to legislation, and it's not too difficult to understand why the owners of the Pentrebach Level and the landowning Squire at the time, were not viewed in a favourable light then or thereafter.

When abandoned the Pentrebach Level and all its appurtenance were left in situ surrounded by a high metal fence attached to which, was a a memorial plaque honouring the sacrifice made by the lost miners. The site was to become a locally hallowed spot.

Ninety-two years later when the National Coal Board proposed opening a new mine in the vicinity of the Pentrebach level it was at first met with strong resistance from the village residents. However, after a compromise of a new memorial plaque containing all the names of the lost miners to be hung in the Pentrebach Miners' Welfare Hall and the NCB's commitment not to encroach upon the old level, the new mine went ahead.

However, after about a year the new mine, due to a historically abnormal geological disturbance, broke into abandoned workings which were found to be those of the old Pentrebach Level. When after further exploration the miners' remains were discovered, the Home Office was notified. However, the suggestion by the Home Office team to keep this discovery and the removal and disposal of the miners' remains a secret, had not bargained with Max Forester, local NUM Chairman.

1

Two men stood at some distance from a high metal fence which had been raised around an abandoned colliery site over ninety years earlier. It was very likely – there being no gateway in the fine mesh fence, standing twelve feet high; its upper portion curved outward the tip of which cut to expose sharp jagged points all along – that no one had crossed this barrier since the time it was raised.

But now, the long standing fence was being torn down with the use of lengths of steel rope attached to heavy haulage machinery.

Tom Bradshaw and William Miller, coal mining engineers, had been appointed by the National Coal Board to oversee the clearance of, not only the perimeter fence but the entire appurtenance associated with this derelict colliery - with the exception of a single brick tower - which had been left in situ since the mine closed in January 1863.

Before the work of dismantling the fence began a large metal plaque, which had been attached to it, was carefully removed. Inscribed upon the plaque was the following:

The Pentrebach Level Disaster

On January 17th 1863 this colliery-Pentrebach Level-was officially abandoned. Due to an explosion presumably caused by the indeterminate ignition of Methane (Firedamp) Gas, the mine was completely lost.

Despite every endeavour, it was officially agreed that the degree of rock which sealed off the main portal was totally impenetrable. Thus, tragically and with profound regret, the lives and bodies of the 25 men and boys employed therein, were irretrievably lost.

R.I.P

It was intended that this memorial plaque would, after the demolition and clearance work was complete, be attached to the remaining brick tower in perpetual memory of and respect for the twenty-five lost miners.

7

The tower was significant, in that it housed the hooter, which on that tragic day signalled the moment of the disaster; its penetrating alarm alerting the nearby village residents of trouble at the mine.

Prior to the removal of the derelict mine's features, there had been a great deal of debate between the local Council Authority, the National Coal Board, and the National Union of Mineworkers, over the proposal to re-work the Pentrebach coal seam. This resulted in a crowded public meeting, attended by top officials of the Council, the NCB and the NUM, held in the Pentrebach Miners' Welfare Hall, where both the case for re-working the seam and any opposition to such a proposition were to be discussed.

The hall was filled in excess of its recommended capacity. Many stood to fill both aisles and those who could not squeeze in stood in the foyer, the door pegged open that they might hear what was going on. The meeting was opened by Leading Councillor Ben Collins.

A short, corpulent man, Ben Collins had that unwarranted air of superiority sometimes allied to those of his standing. With a sharp and suggestive cough he brought the murmuring audience to attention.

"Good evening, let me begin this meeting by asking everyone here to respect all those who will put forward the case for the National Coal Board's proposal to re-open the Pentrebach seam. I appreciate that there are among you those with opposing views and they will be given the opportunity to express them, but I will not tolerate any unruly or disorderly conduct; we are here to discuss the issue and the outcome of this discussion will be considered by the NCB in due course, when it will report back to the Council with its conclusions. If necessary a further meeting will be arranged, when the opportunity to consider the NCBs decision will be given."

Ben Collins continued in the same dignified tone:

"First I would like to introduce the National Coal Board's representatives seated here on the stage. From your left to right they are: Mr ken Gregory, South Wales Coal field Miners' Agent; Mr Jeffrey Maddocks, NCB Geological Surveyor; Mr Elias Wells, NCB Public Relations Officer and Spokes Person; Mr James Cooper, NCB - NUM Coordinator and Mr Simon Wilson, NCB, South Wales, Legal Representative. As you can see from the presence of these high ranking officers, the National Coal Board accepts the very serious and delicate nature of its proposals concerning the Pentrebach issue and I think we should in return respect the presence of its representatives by granting every courtesy due them."

He then turned to his left and approached the four men seated there but with a somewhat indifferent tone, announced their names and status:

"The four men seated on your right of the stage here, with whom you will be familiar are: NUM Representatives: Mr Max Forester, your local NUM Lodge Chairman and Area Convener; Mr Frank Lewis NUM lodge Secretary; Mr Sam Fisher, South Wales Area NUM Delegate and Mr Charles Cornfield, NUM South Wales Area, Legal Representative.

"I am now going to hand the Chair to Mr Elias Wells, who will put the NCB's case for reworking the Pentrebach seam to you. Please do not interrupt him while he relates the details, there will be plenty of time to respond when he concludes."

With this Ben Collins, displaying a continued air of self-importance, took his seat between the two official groups while Mr Elias Wells rose to address the audience.

In contradistinction with Ben Collins, Mr Wells was a thin, tall wiry man who looked a far less imposing figure;

his voice, however, was clear and his speech articulate but his approach rather less officious than that of Ben Collins.

"Good evening Ladies and gentlemen--a number of women from the village were also present--and thank you for attending here tonight. I wish to make it clear that it is my intention to alleviate your concerns, over the right of those poor souls lost in the Pentrebach Level Disaster, to remain undisturbed. The NCB's proposals for re-working what is generally referred to as the Pentrebach seam may not be entirely clear to you. This seam which is correctly described as the Four feet Bluers, is of considerable unworked coal. Operating for no more than one year and bearing in mind the primitive conditions of the time, the original mine made comparatively limited progress; hardly scratching the surface of this abundant seam.

"A geological survey of the area has determined that not only should the NCB be able to extract coal from this seam for many years to come, but will be able to offer employment to many employees for the same duration at a time when, I'm sure you'll agree, jobs are much needed. But, to come to the question I know you are all keen to put to me; why is it necessary to remove the remnants of the old Pentrebach Level and impose upon that locally hallowed spot, in order to work this seam?

"Let me put your minds at rest at once. The company does not intend to intrude upon the actual underground workings. We know that Pentrebach Level entered into Mynydd-y-Graig from the east and as I have said, was in being for about a year. As a result of a serious attempt to enter the mine in order to rescue the men and boys, the mine portal and for some distance therein, illustrates clear evidence of the would-be rescuers' efforts, futile as they proved to be. Given the primitive pillar and stall method of mining and the lack of mechanism of the day, we have been able to calculate with reasonable accuracy, how much progress the mine might have made. Regrettably, no subterranean plans of the mine exist or any details of its progression; probably as a result of the limited progress achieved in a single year; we know for example that no return airway or shaft had been established, had this been the case it's possible that lives might have been saved.

"Believe me we, by which I refer to the National Coal Board as a whole, share your respect and sympathy for those lost in the 1863 disaster, which is why we will be leaving the plaque raised by the people at the time, in recognition of the lost miners' sacrifice, in a prominent position for perpetuity. But there will be a need to clear the area containing the colliery remnants, which have been enclosed since the mine was abandoned; for this is the only practical access point from Mynydd-y-Graig, where a dram road can be run down the mountainside to where a screening plant will be erected.

"The original mine used a weight and gravity-operated endless rope system to raise and lower the drams along this only available route. Now, a little over ninety years later, the NCB intends to adopt a similar contemporary system, as it appears to be the most sensible. To explain the topographical reasons for this I will call upon Mr Jeffery Maddocks, our geologist."

With this Elias Wells took his seat and Jeffrey Maddocks took centre stage. Jeffrey Maddocks looked what he was, an academic. His amply proportioned nose supporting a status fulfilling pince-nez, he leaned forward to consult the notes he had prepared, placed upon a lectern. After a long pause he raised his head and addressed the audience as a school-master might a classroom of students.

"I would first point out that the topography in the region of the old Penterbach mine undulates and is frequently interrupted by minor glacial cirques, caused by the deposits of boulder-clay receding as the ice of the Pleistocene gradually melted. As already pointed out by Mr Wells, appropriating a suitable route down the mountainside to transport the coal to the screening plant and railway sidings; will be determined by adapting the limited causeway originally used by the old Pentrebach Level operatives, who, with considerably progressive thinking for the period, adopted the weight and gravity system which, it is the NCB's intention to replicate."

Suddenly, Max Forester, rose to his feet and interrupted the geologically erudite Mr Maddocks. Forester was a much respected trade unionist by both the men and management; being a fair and considerate negotiator. He was a well-spoken man having had a Grammar school education followed by several years study under the Workers Education Association (WEA) in Trade Unionism and its Laws. A tall man with a mop of bushy hair he had held his position in the Trade Union Movement for many years. Above all he was a plain speaker who did not hold back.

"Enough! Enough!' He bellowed. 'We came here tonight to learn the reasons why the NCB has decided to re-open the Pentrebach seam, not to be subjected to some pompous scholarly lecture. If you people want to explain those reasons in a way they will be understood, then for God's sake get someone up there who can speak in layman's terms. Academics and Professors have their place but it's not here."

With that Ben Collins jumped to his feet.

"You're entirely out of order, Mr Forester, I must ask you to sit down until you are called and let Mr Maddocks continue his excellent explanatory speech, if it's beyond you, perhaps it is you who's in the wrong place."

"Don't you start Ben Collins," Max Forester shouted, "we've had more than enough of your high and mighty attitude, this is a working man's Hall not one of your plush council meeting rooms where you get paid for blabbing all day and coming to no decisions. Let Jim Cooper put forward the case for the NCB, we're all accustomed to his speaking."

Ben Collins, now quite red in the face, was about to embark upon a verbal diatribe against Clive Forester, the two men never having seen eye to eye, when James Cooper voluntarily rose, waving his arms in the air and calling for calm.

"Gentlemen, gentlemen, please, let's not allow the meeting to degenerate into a slanging match in anyone's language. Ben, Clive, simmer down now. Wasn't it you Ben who announced earlier that you would not tolerate any unruly or disorderly conduct?"

Then stepping forward and turning to face the official representatives, he asked if anyone objected to his taking the floor, at the same time apologising to Jeffrey Maddocks who had sat down out of contempt. As no one seemed to object and as Ben Collins and Max Forester had resumed their seats, mumbling abuses at one another, James Cooper turned to the audience and began to speak.

"First I would like to thank the previous speakers whose intentions, I'm sure, were genuine and who were making every endeavour to put the NCB's case forward in their particular style. And I feel certain that most of you will have got the gist of the Coal Board's intended plans. I think we can safely say, however, that the difficulty as far as you village residents are concerned, cannot be found in geology or topography but in the very human objection to any encroachment upon a site, which has become a place sacred to the memory of those poor souls lost in the Pentrebach disaster."

There followed a loud applause of approval which, when it subsided, brought in its wake an atmosphere of calm.

James Cooper continued.

"I have studied in detail the plans for the proposed new mine and feel bound to say that the NCB has, indeed, taken great pains not to intrude upon the location of the original mine. Nevertheless, the plans do clearly illustrate that to locate a site where operations for establishing the necessary buildings for a new mine, without the removal of the remnants of the old works, would be impractical. I fully appreciate there will be residents among you of Pentrebach village, who will have lost ancestral family members in the 1863 disaster and this makes it more difficult for them to accept any proposals for a new mine in the vicinity of that terrible tragedy. The Pentrebach explosion created a rare situation in that none of the miners were saved; the complete collapse of the mine meant that, despite all efforts, rescue was impossible.

"But, while I am convinced that there is no one here who does not harbour respect, sorrow and a deep sense of loss towards the victims and relatives of this appalling tragedy; we must nonetheless move on."

17

There was a groan of disapproval from some of the audience in response to this last remark and one man raised his hand and appealed to the Chair to be allowed to respond.

Ben Collins got up, once again exercising his role as Chairman, and announced that he believed the order of the meeting's programme was already being breached. To which Max Forester responded with:

"To hell with the programme Ben Collins, let the man have his say while his train of thought is fresh."

This brought a degree of disharmony among the crowd, which was quickly quelled by James Cooper, who pointed out that the gentleman who wished to respond to his comments was the vicar of Capel Pentre, and that he would be more than happy to hear what he has to say.

Reverend Desmond Thorn was a sixty-eight year old man who had not only lived in Pentrebach village all his life but his great grandfather's brother, Sam Thorn had been lost in the Pentrebach Level disaster. The Reverend was a very popular figure and his chapel was still well attended by many in the village, although his congregation was nowadays predominantly female.

Sporting a full head of white hair over a very friendly face and a calm pleasant speaking voice; people, even those who did not attend the church, generally liked him.

"Mr Cooper speaks of moving on and I find no fault in progress," the Reverend began. "But with regard to this particular issue I think we should consider leaving the Pentrebach site as it is and as it has been since the year of the disaster; in other words allowing this particular piece of history to not move on. Why do I believe this to be the best outcome? Because there is evidence to suggest that the decision to leave the entire colliery appurtenances in situ, was unanimously agreed by the then society: villagers, mineworkers and mine and land owners in view of the special circumstances of this tragedy where none of the workmen could be saved nor one body recovered."

With that the minister sat down and James Cooper resumed his place.

"Thank you Reverend Thorn," he began, "you have clearly expressed your view on the subject and I am sure there are many like-minded people in the audience. However, I must contend that you may be laying too much emphasis upon just how far we should continue to go in marking this sad event of so long ago. Yes, of course we should remember the tragedy and honour the memory of all those who died that terrible day. Yes, of course there should be a suitable epitaph and there is. But to continue to sanctify, guard and preserve the entire Pentrebach colliery site for posterity seems to me to be a little over-attentive."

Again there were some disapproving murmurs among the audience but they were less pronounced than when earlier, James Cooper had suggested it was time to move on.

"What I would suggest, if I may," James Cooper continued, "is that a plaque of remembrance and recognition – including a list of the names of all those lost in the disaster, if available - be raised here in this Miners' Welfare Hall, where it can be seen by all the villagers for generations to come. How many of you have ever visited the Pentrebach colliery site to read the original testimony? Not many I would suggest. It is, after all, some way above the village and not nowadays, easily reached."

This proposition was greeted with a somewhat surprising resounding applause. James Cooper had, unwittingly, come up with an idea that seemed to gain favour all round. Even the Reverend Thorn nodded his approval, and when the clapping had abated, rose to his feet for a second time, and announced:

"I must congratulate you Mr Cooper on an excellent suggestion; bringing the story of this unprecedented disaster into the village proper must make sense and I feel confident that, along with me, all Capel Pentre's members will give it unanimous support."

As this obvious acquiescence on the part of the vicar made for a more or less mutual seal of approval with regard to the two opposing views, there was a moment's pause in the proceedings when Max Forester rose and beckoned to the Chair to be heard. His request was granted.

"I wholeheartedly agree with Jim Cooper's suggestion and am very pleased that it has been generally accepted. Perhaps a show of hands might help to confirm this."

Ben Collins, not wishing to be excluded from this mood of general consent, stood up and called for the show of hands proposed by Max Forester, which was taken and illustrated unanimous approval.

Max Forester had not sat down – allowing time for the confirming interruption - and called upon Ben Collins, as

Leader of the Council, to take responsibility along with his colleagues, for the making of the proposed plaque.

"I can assure you Mr Forester, responded Ben Collins, "that the council will, indeed, take responsibility for producing this memorial plaque. Let us hope that the names of all the victims can be found among the archival records; I must once again congratulate Mr Cooper for his excellent suggestion."

"And I," Max Forester announced, "am confident that every member of the Lodge and Welfare Committee along with every mineworker and village resident will be more than happy to see the plaque raised in this Miners' Welfare Hall, well done Jim Cooper."

With this Ben Collins brought the meeting to a close satisfied that it had run much more smoothly than he could have hoped. He had anticipated some bitter interchanges and had expected there to be no amicable conclusion. Instead, thanks to James Cooper, a very happy and unanimously harmonious conclusion had been achieved. There will, he conjectured, be no need for a further meeting; the NCB would be able to go ahead without more ado.

And Ben Collins' conjecture proved to be the case. The decision to remove the old mine's appurtenance, excepting the old tower, and the re-working of the four feet Bluers seam, witnessed no further objections. The new commemorative plaque which, after a thorough archival investigation included all the victims' names, was raised in a prominent position in the Pentrebach Miners' Welfare Hall, to everyone's delight.

2

Within weeks the two National Coal Board engineers, Tom Bradshaw and William Miller, arrived at the scene of the old mine to superintend the demolition project. The month was September the year 1955, ninety-two years since the old Pentrebach mine closed. The entire operation was complete within a few more weeks and all that remained – as formerly agreed - was the old brick tower with the original metal plaque of remembrance attached in a prominent position thereon.

The portal of the old mine, sealed as it was by a solid wall of rock, showed visible signs of the determined effort made to reach the trapped miners. Given the available tools of the time the would-be rescuers had penetrated a considerable way into the mine before the sheer resistance of the rock made any further progress possible. There was clear evidence of the use of dynamite – a last resort – considering the risk of a further explosion - especially not knowing whether the men might still be alive but trapped within. But, alas, this too had proven ineffective. It was at this spot that both engineers now stood examining the face of the rock which had sealed the fate of those twenty-five men and boys all those years ago.

"Gives you an eerie feeling standing here Will, doesn't it?" Tom suggested.

"Yes, Tom, it does, all throughout these few weeks we've been working here, I must admit I've been unable to get the tragedy out of my mind, especially when I look to the top of that old tower and see that hooter casting its trumpet-like cone out into the air; I half expect it to blast out its siren call. Crazy isn't it?

"From what I observed before the clearance began, it was obvious that this was an innovative mine for its time," continued Will. "They were using a steam-powered haulage to pull the drams out from underground for instance, when many were still using horses. Of course steam power had been used to pump water from mines as early as the seventeenth century but small undertakings like this would not generally be so advanced; the weight and gravity incline was also forward thinking for the 1860s. They must have had bigger plans for this mine, all sadly lost after just one year by this sudden disaster. They did use horses or probably cobs (ponies) of course, to pull the drams from the stalls to the main dram road but then the steam haulage took over."

"The accident is still something of a mystery though Will," said Tom, "no one really knows what happened.

By all accounts those working on the surface heard an explosion coming from the mine portal followed by a ball of fire which quickly dissipated; witnesses claimed that the mouth of the mine totally disappeared under the collapse of the top and that was that."

"Apparently, from what is recorded in the minutes of the official Hearing," interjected Will, "the steam haulage operator claimed that the rope attached to the journey, in this mine, no more than six drams, suddenly stopped and he was unable to continue the process of withdrawal. He applied the haulage break and waited for the Repairer to signal him. But within seconds the explosion occurred followed by a ball of fire and the mine caved in. It was he who set the hooter in motion; operated by compressed air alongside a fan used to force air into the mine – as a return airway or shaft had not yet been driven - to improve ventilation. Though given its dimensions I doubt that this fan would have proved very effective. Both the fan and the hooter, as you say, were contained within the old brick tower, which we have left standing. The operating controls, however, were in the winding house."

"What puzzles me Will," stressed Tom, "is why they had not cut a return airway or shaft?

"Remember now Tom," explained Will, "the mine was only operating for one year, at that time profit was the all-important aim. The overall value of the new mine would have been considered before embarking on the job of commencing with a major non-profit operation as constructing a return airway or shaft would have been. I understand that at the Hearing the failure to cut the return airway or shaft was deemed "unfortunate" and "regrettable" but not negligent or unlawful on the part of the management. Apparently a Fault had occurred which caused a considerable delay in production and this too put the cutting of an air return on hold. It was also declared that a team of experienced men (hard-heading workers) were just finishing a job in a neighbouring valley and were to begin work on Pentrebach return airway next. It was conjectured, with no evidence to prove otherwise, that it was likely that the entire mine had, in fact, been lost under the fall, consequently, the cutting of any airway would have proved irrelevant."

"This must illustrate the power of the Squires in those days Will. No court was going to find the Lord of the Manor negligent now were they?"

"Actually Tom, "the Squire's role was not in question. Despite the colliery being on his land, by this time, it would have been leased along with the mineral rights to others who would take full responsibility for its management and operation. Nevertheless, the Squire would, of course, benefit financially as a non-participating shareholder, receiving a handsome percentage of the profits."

"Well, sadly, without survivors, Will," stressed Tom, "it's very unlikely that we will ever know exactly what happened. By the way they've got the hooter working again, operated by electricity this time, but I'm sure no one will be anxious to hear it."

And on that melancholy note the two men left the scene to descend the mountain.

3

Pentrebach (little village) came into existence along with other similar groups of terraced cottages throughout Cwm-yr-Afon-Gwen (Valley of the White River), as a result of the development of a number of small coal mines. The original inhabitants had been pastoral farmers living a very modest existence. At that time their cottages were scattered and built by traditional needs; sturdy stone structures able to withstand the weather and time without the need of change. Each farm throughout the valley would be self-sufficient -i.e. supplying a family's basic needs. Sheep were by far the predominant means of income with perhaps some poultry and a few pigs.

The farmers were tenant farmers who leased their land and property from one of the three Landed Gentry – referred to as Squires- who owned tracts of land throughout the valley. The tenants were also duty bound to pay tithe (one tenth of their income) to the parish church. As a result of these obligations these tenant families were markedly impoverished but, without any other source of income – the land being poorly suited for agricultural or horticultural purpose, save for a few domestic vegetables - they were left to make the best of their limited resources.

By the end of the eighteenth century a few small coal mines had been opened on either side of the valley by those enterprising Squires, who now began to appreciate that there was a more lucrative living to be made from the coal industry than that obtained solely from leasing out the farms.

However, at first there was some difficulty in getting enough local men to work in the mines; descending from hundreds of years of farming stock these were outdoor people, the very idea of working beneath the land was not readily appealing. Nonetheless, the Squires began to persuade many of the younger farm-hands to forsake their traditional occupation by offering them an independent wage and a place to live. A further inducement came about, when the Squires began to encourage Irish labourers to come to the valley to fill the vacant jobs and houses, a practice which became common as the years went by and the Irish settlers more welcome. This pressure along with the incentives might have convinced the younger farmers to make the break with tradition but it only incensed the more entrenched heads of the families, who stood to lose not just their labour but their family at the same time.

A young boy raised on a farm became part of that farm's working complement; he was expected to apply himself to the running of the farm and work alongside his father and brothers to the exclusion of all else. He would not be paid, as such, but would have his board and lodge found and when old enough, a little money to join the other men and other young lads at the ale house.

His life, however, was entirely committed to his family and the farm and this would involve a round-the-clock obligation. His only 'escape' would be to marry and with the help of his family and the bride's family, set up a place of his own. He would invariably marry one of the girls from a neighbouring farm as apart from the once a week visit to the town market, he would have little opportunity to come into contact with any girl from outside the valley.

It was this chance to break away from their restricted lives, not overlooking the other incentives, that helped encourage the young farmers to turn to coal mining as a way of earning an independent living and, because they would be no longer bound to the farm, a much more liberal existence. As the Squires began to develop small settlements here and there along the valley floor, to house their gradually-increasing labour force, so, more and more of the younger farmers abandoned their traditional working lives for the mines and an independent settled home in which to live.

By the early years of the nineteenth century a canal was cut along the length of the valley to convey the ever increasing coal output to the port - set at the principal town harbour - for distribution country wide. Coal mining and not pastoral farming was now the dominant industry.

With the gradual loss of their sons, some of the older farmers were, reluctantly, also being forced to turn to mining. Inevitably, there were a number of true traditionalists who were still unable to make the transition and carried on with wives and daughters substituting, as best they could, for the departed sons; but they were now very much in the minority. Some of them, enterprisingly, helped subsidise their income by leasing horses to the mine owners and/or the canal company. And yet others, who were not prepared to work in the mines; come what may, but accepted that their farming days were numbered, engaged in diverse occupations such as: Inn Keepers, cobblers, barbers, etc. So, as time went on, inevitably, most of the farms were abandoned altogether and allowed to fall into disrepair and gradual decay.

For many years those living in the little groups of terraced houses known as Pentrebach, worked in one or other of the small mines further up or down the valley.

In January 1862 however, a new mine was opened entering the higher slope of Mynydd-y-Graig and was to take its name from the little settlement below, thus Pentrebach Level was created. It wasn't long before the men already living in Pentrebach were given the option to transfer to the new mine; an understanding between the then relevant owners being agreed, to facilitate the transfers. Not all, by any means, accepted this transfer offer, most preferring to work in an established mine they were familiar with, aware that the early years of a mine's development could sometimes be fraught with unexpected anomalies.

From the beginning of the century up to the 1862 opening of the Pentrebach Level, the village had been gradually developing; now there were several streets of terraced houses, an Inn, General Stores and Communal Bakehouse, where anyone could take their bread to be baked and a Barbers-cum-Cobblers. It was near Pentrebach that the ancient valley church of St Catwg stood and as the village grew so the people living there took to calling it Capel Pentre and the name stuck.

About two miles from Pentrebach was Afon Manor House the home of Squire William Watkins and his family. The Watkins' known ancestry went back over four hundred years, the Manor having progressed from a Yeoman's farm to the very noble edifice of the day. Forty-three year old William Watkins was the owner of the Estate upon which the new mine at Pentrebach and a number of other mines were located, which covered a large portion of the upper valley, two other Squires: George Carew and Richard Lewis shared the remainder of the valley land. It was the forefathers of these landed gentry who had invested in the cutting of the valley canal and the opening of the early coal mines. But as time went by Landed Gentry, as with the three Squires (an epithet which was becoming less familiar) while they never lost the right of landlords, were no longer engaged in the practical running of the coal mines, assuming the role of silent beneficiaries.

It was the independent Owner/Shareholders -based at Cardiff- who held the control and governing of the coal mines. While General Managers, Mining Engineers, Chief Clerks and Cashiers - involved in the day-to-day running of the coal mines – might also have a financial stake in their colliery, which encouraged their committment to its success.

The Squires' lack of practical involvement in the mines did not, however, diminish their control over the lives of the miners, as they continued to own the miners' dwellings, the General Stores, the several Inns and by way of obligation, the miners and their families too.

Of course there was never any social intercourse between the miners' families and those of the Manor Houses; their societies being so grossly removed from one another. Whenever a carriage or pony and fly, belonging to the Watkins' household would pass through Pentrebach, a slight bow of the head or a gentle tip of a hat would, by any who might be at the roadside at the time, to some degree confirm their accepted subordinate status.

In order that he need have no direct contact with working class families, Squire Watkins – as with all others of his standing - employed numerous people to oversee and administer his Estate affairs. The most important of these was the Estate Bailiff. It was the Bailiff who collected the cottage rents and the profits from the Estate shops and Inn. The shop keepers and Inn keeper were paid a wage in proportion to their respective profits, which was never going to make them rich; if profits were good they would be paid a reasonable wage, if, on the other hand, profits were not so good, their income would reflect this. It was, therefore, in their interests to establish a good rapport with their customers, though most had little option other than to use the Inn and Stores in close proximity to their homes.

The Bailiff was also responsible for maintaining the Estate laws, those of trespass for instance. Should anyone be found on the 'private' areas of the Estate or, more seriously, poaching fish from that part of the river running through the Estate or snaring rabbits in the Estate woods, they would be dealt with severely. Crimes such as stealing apples, blackberries or mushrooms, from the Estate land, were also offences punishable by a trip to the Quarter Sessions and suffering the unpleasant consequences, which in extreme circumstances – repeat offences for example – could lead to a loss of a job or even eviction from the company house.

Apart from the Bailiff there were a number of other people employed on the Estate; several Gardeners under a Head Gardener; a Woodward, whose job it was to keep the woods and fencing in good order and report to the Bailiff any evidence of poaching or rabbit snaring. At the stables there was an Ostler –who was more often than not also the Blacksmith- and Grooms and young lads to keep the stables clean and feed the horses. There was, of course a Coachman, always ready to take any members of the family to wherever they may wish to journey. Well-to-do families like the Watkins would have a family carriage (a landau or a curricle) in use whenever the family needed to travel some distance. Other, less pretentious vehicles were also kept for the use of one or two people to travel short distances, for example a fly or a gig; usually drawn by a pony or small horse.

Of course the house would have the customary working staff: a cook and her assistants, a butler and a number of man-servants and the various house maids and female attendants.

It was only during the church service on Sunday that most of the villagers ever saw the Squire and his wife (Margaret) and family: son Rees and two daughters: Mary and Jane, and then only from a distance. There was a strict order of entry to the church; the Manor House family arriving in their carriage would be guided by the vicar or his curate to their private pews, before any of the villagers were even allowed to enter the church precincts.

While many of the Pentrebach men worked in collieries some distance from the village, some had nonetheless turned down the offer to transfer to the newly opened Pentrebach Level, for the reason already referred to. Nevertheless, the General Managers had no difficulty in obtaining a full complement of workers, including some Irish immigrants, as the mine did not need as many workers as a long-established mine would.

4

Talk of the new mine was very much the topic in and around the village and especially in Pentrebach Inn, where some of those who were and some of those who were not moving, sat around a table drinking and debating their different views on the subject. On this particular night several men were gathered together, along with Tom Bishop and his son Ben

"'ow long'll it take before the new mine opens, then dad?" questioned Ben.

"Oh! The 'ard-'eading boys will have to drive in 'til they reach the coal seam first my boy, and that'll take a few weeks no doubt."

"Who are these 'ard-'eading boys, then dad?"

"They're independent workers Ben, who come in whenever a mine needs openin' or to drive the Main or airway on, in a workin' mine. It's not only 'ard work it's skilled work too, my boy. Notchin' a pair of timber so as the joints are tight takes experience. Later, when the mine is up and runnin' the Repairer will take over the maintenance. There was an old Repairer, Dan Cooper, in the Holy-bush years ago, who could notch a pair of timber so as 'u couldn't see no light through the joints.

'ow well the 'ard 'eading boys drive and support the Main can make all the difference. A badly cut and supported Main makes for an unsafe mine."

Tom Bishop was in his forties and had worked underground since he was eleven years of age and had collected many blue scars to verify it. Now he and his twenty-two year old son Ben had signed an agreement to move from the Holly-bush Level, on land owned by Squire Richard Lewis, to the new Pentrebach Level as soon as it opens, as they lived in Miners' Terrace, Pentrebach. Moving to the new mine would mean just a half-hour trek up the mountainside instead of well over an hour and a half to the Holy-bush; and a lot quicker coming home.

"U an' u're two boys are movin' with us aren't 'u Wally?" Ben asked, addressing Wally Jones from Watkins Row.

"Aye, that's right, Ben, we 'ave signed up." Wally replied. "They're lettin' so many go from different mines in the valley but no more than three or four from each mine. Quite a few 'ave turned it down mind 'u, but the Managers 'ave agreed not to force noone who don't want to move."

Wally's two boys were Ken and Brian, who were fifteen and fourteen respectively.

"They tell me," broke in Will Simmons, -who lived next door to the Bishops and who was not moving to the new mine- "that that Bluers seam 'olds a lot of firedamp, 'ave 'u' 'eard anythin' about that Tom?"

"Now then Will," said Tom Bishop, "no bloody scaremongerin' 'u don't want to frighten my lad before he starts now do 'u?"

"I'm just tellin' 'u what I 'eard Tom, lots of mines have firedamp, but it is more common in bituminous seams, bindin' coal as we call it, like the Bluers, that's all I'm sayin'. Anyway I'm sure they'll have more than enough canaries standin' by to let 'u know when the gas is about." He joked.

Everyone knew what he was referring to, even young Ben, but he was not as keen to join in his humour.

"Well now Will, the Old Ivy Level – where Will Simmons and his two sons worked – is also bindin' coal as 'u know," said Tom quickly. "In fact most levels are; it's generally the deeper pits that have anthracite but even there 'u could find firedamp. It depends more on clean air; good ventilation in other words, and these things are improvin' all the time so if there's any new system comin' out, there's a good chance we'll have it in the new mine. Mind 'u' the Holy-bush 'as far as I know, 'as only had one small gas explosion in twenty years, so things are not as bad as 'u're makin' it out to be Will Simmons."

"Well, I never 'eard of any explosions in the Old Ivy Level and certainly none since I've been there, which is why me and my boys are 'appy to stay where we are," Will Simmons declared.

Thankfully, Tom was pleased to find no more was said that evening about firedamp or canaries, for that matter.

Ben, however, had continued to think about it and approached his father when they got home, about firedamp and its dangers.

"U've been workin' underground for eight years now, Ben, so 'u're experienced enough to know that minin' is a dangerous job. Like me 'u've seen a few boys injured and a couple killed too; remember Sam Wilks and Tony Craven under that fall a couple of years back, but no gas explosions. Firedamp is just one of the risks we take but it's a rare risk, far more colliers are injured and killed by falls than ever through firedamp, so just 'u' be careful with 'u're timberin' my boy and 'u'll be alright. And don't 'u go worryin' about the likes of Will Simmons, he just likes to feel important."

'Righto Dad, I won't let it bother me no more." Ben replied, but secretly he was still troubled.

For the next few months the village was abuzz with gossip in anticipation of the new mine opening. Then someone dropped two letters through 4 Miners' Terrace, one addressed to Tom Bishop and one to his son Ben. They were from the Colliery General Manager, informing them both that on Monday next, they were to report to the lower end of the gravity haulage at the new mine, where they will receive their instructions.

Soon letters began dropping in at a number of other Pentrebach cottages – at the Jones family home in Watkins Row for instance- with the same intent. The news very quickly spread that the miners who had applied to move to the new Pentrebach Level had received their instructions; there were to be a few boys among them.

The letters (including an Agreement to be signed by each employee) had informed the men and boys of their commitment and duties and of their rates of pay and the general rules that they would be obliged to adhere to. Most of this Agreement conformed to the standard practices, which were not dissimilar throughout the whole valley; care was taken not to give favour – not that there was much by way of favour anyway - to any one mine over another and thereby give cause for discontent.

On the first day the men had gathered together at the foot of the endless rope ready to make their way up to the mine. On this one occasion they were given permission to jump into any of the six empty drams to be carried up to the colliery site. Because they were already established miners, each man had his own set of tools purchased at his own expense from the Company store. Collectively these would have been too heavy to carry all the way up to the mine so the company had made an exception and allowed them and their tools to make the journey this way. Because it was necessary to have full drams in order to haul the empties up, six drams of stone had been made ready for the purpose.

Despite all the information being laid down in their written contract, it was still necessary for the Overman, on the day of opening, to gather all the men and boys at the colliery site to enlighten them as to how they would be expected to work in this particular mine.

"Good mornin' Lads, my name is Steve Parfitt and I am the colliery Overman. I will be in overall charge and it is to me that 'u must come if 'u 'ave anythin' to ask. The two men to my left, Clive Harding and Eddie Jones, are the appointed Shotsmen and it is only they who 'ave the authority to fire any coal or road; bottom and top, they will also be actin' as Deputies and will report any problems that may arise, to me. But I know I'm dealing with experienced miners 'ere today, so I don't anticipate no difficulties, though I am prepared to make certain allowances for a settlin' in period; let's say one week. I'll begin with a roll-call and then explain a few things 'u should know about this particular mine."

With the roll-call addressed and found to be correct, Steve Parfitt began to explain the way the mine was to operate.

"The mine 'as been made ready by the 'ard-'eading workers and so 'ave all the branch roads to the stalls; butties or family members who worked together in their last job can do so 'ere wherever possible.

"We have two good 'Aliars' (a colloquial used to describe the men who handled the ponies underground, probably derived from 'hauliers', the spelling of which is conjectural) they are behind me 'ere and 'u can get to know um later on. They will keep 'u supplied with drams and take them away when they are full. Always mark your drams; an unmarked dram will not be counted and, therefore, not paid for. You will 'ave to push the drams out from the stalls but the ponies, small cobs as they are, will take 'um back to the double-partin' where after every six drams 'ave been brought out and coupled, they will be hauled to the surface by steam haulage. Each dram will then be clipped onto the endless rope and lowered down the mountain; at the bottom of the incline we 'ave a tippin' table and 'Billy Fairplay' (for separating the small from the large coal) and then the coal will be taken away by trucks from the railway sidin's." By the time the Pentrebach Level opened the canal had been superseded by the development of a railway along the valley floor, opened in 1855.

"I can tell 'u boys 'u are now workin' in an up to date mine. The water from the deep, is pumped out by a steam operated pump so 'u needn't worry about that. We believe the coal in this mine is pretty soft, or at least it is at the moment, so 'u might get away with only 'oling out. However, should 'u need to fire the coal, 'u will bore the 'ole or 'oles and gather the clay for rammin', but only either Clive or Eddie will put the powder in and fill a 'ole and fire. When firin', everyone must leave the area and not return until the smoke is clear; all 'oles fired and time taken must be registered in the Shotsman's duty book.

"Just across the way from us is, as 'u can see, the stables where we keep four cobs The Aliars will take the cobs down every morning and bring 'um out at the end of the shift; no one else is to 'andle the cobs.

"Well, that's about it for now Lads', said the Overman, 'welcome to Pentrebach Level, let's hope we can all work together and get on."

5

The old tin bath was set close to the fire and filled with hot water, heated in a large metal pot over an open fire. May Bishop had been busy with this task, while her mother, Gwladys, was attending to the meal, in preparation for Tom and Ben's arrival home after their first shift at the new Pentrebach Level.

"I 'ope things 'ave gone right for 'um today May', said her mother. 'It's always difficult when 'u' start in a new place."

"Dad and Ben are used to it tho' Mam, aren't they. Same thing they'll be doing, i'n'it Mam?"

"Aye, the same job, but all mines are not the same mind 'u May; it could be very dusty or very wet or the coal might be hard or soft and besides that, there are lots of things, May bach, that me and 'u will never understand, that can make for a good or a bad colliery, let's wait and see my gel."

Soon Tom and Ben trudged in and were allowed to have their bath, in a part of the room sectioned off by a large hanging curtain, where the tin bath of steaming water stood, and then settle down to their meal, before the barrage of questions about their first shift, from both Gwladys and May, dominated the conversation.

Between mouthfuls Tom and Ben tried to answer their questions but whether either of the women really understood how their day had gone, remained unclear. It wasn't that that mattered anyway, it was their genuine concern.

It wasn't just the Bishops, of course, who were coming home from that first shift at the new mine. A number of houses in each of the several terraced streets of Pentrebach village were also opening doors to welcome weary men or boys in after their first day. Among them, Wally, Ken and Brian Jones for instance, who were also getting the third degree from the women folk.

Here however, it was rather different as the two boys were so much younger. Ken was only fifteen and Brian just fourteen. Ken had perhaps been luckier than Brian as he had been allowed to work with his father. Brian had been placed with Walter Jones-not related-who was an experienced collier but was given a boy helper because of his age. This was not an uncommon practice. As a collier reached the age of fifty plus he might find the work getting a little too much for him. To admit this, however, could cost him his job or, there being one available, being moved to a less demanding job; the down side of this was a considerable loss in wages. It was the luckier ones, therefore, who were allocated a boy to help ease the load and this was the case with Walter Jones who was fifty-two.

"How did old Wally Jones treat 'u then Bri'?" His father asked. "He's not a bad old sort mind 'u, 'u do your bit and 'u should be alright with 'im my boy."

"It was O. K. dad, 'cept the curlin' box kept gettin' stuck on the bottom. Wally made sure we 'ad plenty of posts up tho' with the top bein' as it is; 'Safety first young Brian.' He kept saying.

"Aye, 'u'll be alright with 'im my boy." His father confirmed.

Whatever the men told their families, one thing was for sure; they were all glad to see that first shift over and Tom Bishop upon reflection, was even unsure whether he had made the right decision in moving to the new mine. Certain things he had noticed about the mine had given him rise for concern. Nonetheless, any doubts he might have were kept to himself; it wouldn't do to upset Ben by suggesting that the move might not have been as wise as he had first thought.

Of the streets that went to make up the little village of Pentrebach, one was called Riverside Row - for obvious reasons - which consisted of 'back-to-back' houses, where the party wall run down the centre of the buildings the whole length of the street, creating separate dwellings either side. Despite running alongside a different road, both sides of the terrace were called Riverside Row, although most people living in Pentrebach referred to them as 'back-to-backs' preceded by the appropriate number. The numbers one to ten run up one side –close to the river- and eleven to twenty down the other. Due to the method of construction these dwellings offered poor and limited accommodation; just one room up and one room down. Nevertheless, it was amazing how many could live in such cramped conditions; sometimes families with three or even four children.

There were three Irish families living in numbers seven, eight and nine respectively. At number seven Shaun O'Grady and his wife Kathleen, and their three children aged from one year to twelve; at number eight Michael Donovan and his wife Caroline and their three children aged from three to nine and at number nine, Jeremiah O'Conner and his wife Mavis and their two children aged four and five years.

The three Irish men all now worked in the new Pentrebach Level, O'Grady and O'Connor having transferred from the Holy-bush and Donovan from the Old Ivy. These Irish families were very much a part of the established community.

Miners' Terrace and Watkins Row, to name but two of the other streets, which were much longer streets than Riverside Row, were regarded as standard miners' cottages; two rooms downstairs, one living room and a smaller scullery - more often than not referred to as the 'back' kitchen - and two bedrooms upstairs. Where there were more than two or three children, the bedrooms would be partitioned using a large curtain to create more sleeping space, a bedroom might also have a 'crogloft' – much more common in the older farm dwellings - where half the room had a raised platform, access to which would be gained by a removable ladder. This would provide extra sleeping space, especially for young children. Sometimes the living room would be divided with the clever use of the larger furniture giving the impression of two separate rooms. In the case of the back-to-backs, all manner of makeshift partitions and 'croglofts' were utilised to create divisions between the adults and the children and between older girls and boys, when necessary.

Lavatories were always outside, usually at the bottom of the garden and the toilet buckets removed daily, to be emptied into a stream that ran through the centre of the village; often the job of the children or wives; a permanent sewage system not yet achieved. Such insanitary practices sometimes resulted in the spread of diseases such as Typhoid or even Cholera.

Apart from the daily task of emptying the toilet buckets, children would play along the banks of the contaminated stream; floating matchsticks under a rickety bridge that connected one part of the village with another or during a hot summer even bathing their feet to keep cool. The banks of this same stream were home the common water rat and other unsavoury rodents; exposing these children to the risk of infection.

There had been a serious outbreak of cholera in the Welsh valleys in the late 1840s when in some cases whole families succumbed to this terrible disease. Therefore, child mortality was high – not just in Pentrebach of course but in all other similar villages - it was not uncommon for large families, to lose one or two children before they reached puberty.

The Pentrebach Inn, owned by Squire Watkins and managed by Ted Morgan, was at the end of Miners' Terrace and the Company Stores, taking up the space of two houses, in the centre. The communal Bakehouse was at the end of Watkins Row and at the other end in one room, was the Barbers-cum-Cobblers. This was run by Sammy Jones who had decided to pursue these skills when he was forced to give up his farm, being determined not to work underground. But the premises were of course, owned by the Squire. As the title suggests the Company Stores was also owned by Squire Watkins and catered for almost everything a miner's family might need. The thing about any of the Company Stores throughout the valley, or in any mining community for that matter, was that they obligated the mining families to use them, thereby tightening control of the Squires over them.

However, Squire Watkins did not operate the "truck system" at the stores or the Inn, where miners would be part paid with tokens only exchangeable at the Company's outlets; a common practice in many other mining villages and towns at the time, despite an Act prohibiting it –unless by agreement- passed as early as 1831. This Act was succeeded by two others, one in 1887 and the other, which finally brought this unpopular practice to an end in 1896.

By and large the early days at the new mine went by without any unexpected difficulties. These were all long-term miners, used to working hard and dealing with the pressures common to their job. Certain things had been noticed however, that clearly illustrated that 'new' as the mine may be, the conditions were all too familiar. The headroom in the Main was low and uneven, the coal seam was wet and the shale top given to shredding, which was a constant worry; making it, as Tom Bishop had told his boy Ben at the pub, necessary to "be careful with 'u're timberin'." But the Overman's reference to soft coal had proved to be true. Consequently, as yet, there had been no need to fire any coal. The two 'Aliars' Ivor Williams and Bill Evans were up to the job, so no one had had to wait long for a change of dram.

Apart from working the coal, colliers were expected to continually drive the road on leading to their stall, and lay the road-rails as they progressed. The coal was turned back from the face by shovel from man to man – there were always two in a stall- or a man and a young boy helper – a shovel of coal would be too heavy for a younger boy, so he would use a curling box, which looked much like a coal scuttle. He would scoop the coal up and push the curling box to the edge of the road to tip it into the dram, set on the road level with the bottom of the coalface. The section of shale and clod (known as bottom) had to be fired and removed every time the road needed to catch up with the face. Occasionally, due to natural pressure, the roof (referred to as the top) would also have to be fired and the debris removed. The colliers were paid by yardage –though not very generously- when removing bottom or top but sometimes the shale and clod was mixed with heavy stone or clay making progress much more difficult. There was no extra paid for this and by and large it cost the colliers both time and money.

One of the first things the colliers noticed about this mine was that it was subject to heavy natural pressure, which they called 'a squeeze.' One of the effects of a squeeze was that from time to time the ground beneath the dram-road, which they may only have laid a few weeks earlier, would lift up and cause the rails to shift out of line. This had to be attended to quickly, making it necessary to remove a length of rail and cut away the offending protruding ground - known in Welsh as 'pwcyns'- and relay the rails. This extra work for which they were not paid, was very unpopular, creating an unnecessary delay and a subsequent loss of earnings.

Evidence of the squeeze problem could even be seen in the Main, which normally, due to its distance from the coal face, was rarely affected by such pressure. Tom Bishop spoke of the 'disturbance,' above and between the pairs of timber - erected by the hard-heading workers when driving the mine to the face - to Steve Parfitt but the Overman dismissed it as "Just the top settlin' down, Tom, this is a new mine after all."

As the new level progressed and the miners became more familiar with it, it was found to be not unlike any of the other mines at which they had previously worked. The steam haulage and the endless rope might be innovative extras but they had little or no effect upon the conditions down at the coal face; the stalls were low –especially so during a squeeze- and wet. While the men used oil-wick lamps attached to their cloth caps, because they afforded poor light and often went out without warning, tallow candles had to be placed here and there to compensate; they were fitted into a round piece of metal with a spike which could be stuck into the coal or piece of wood to make secure. In fact, lighting or the lack of it was the biggest problem in such dark and confined conditions. Safety lamps (Davey Lamp 1815) which were used to test for gas were only carried by the Deputies but were not designed to afford much light anyway.

6

At home little or nothing had changed for the Bishops or any of the other Pentrebach Level workers and their families. Village life went on much as it always had done, with the husbands and working sons spending up to sixteen hours a day in the mine and the wives and daughters keeping house and making sure there was plenty of hot water with food on the table, when the workers came home.

The backs of Miners' Terrace and the backs of Watkins Row abutted upon one another at the ends of long gardens. This made for easy communication between the two streets and between neighbours on both sides; many, who were either related or just good friends, had gates giving access between the sides and where the ends of the gardens met.

The Bishop family had such a connection between them and the Llewellyns of Watkins Row. Sid Llewellyn and his wife Susan, whose daughter Mabel was courting Ben Bishop, were very good friends of Tom and Gwladys; Sid worked in the next stall to Tom and Ben at the mine. Unlike Tom, Sid did not have a son working with him but did have a boy; fifteen year old Clive Baker. Clive Baker also lived in Watkins Row with his parents and four sisters. Clive's father was Dewi Baker, who operated the steam haulage at Pentrebach Level.

Late on a July Sunday evening – their only day off – a couple of months after the new mine had opened, we find Sid Llewellyn and Tom Bishop chatting at the gate adjoining the bottom of their long gardens.

"'ow'r 'u Tom, I see your runner beans are lookin' good there?"

"Well the Weather's not been too bad, Sid, so the veg' is comin' along tidy. Yours are lookin' pretty good as well mind 'u."

"Not as good as yours Tom; 'u 'aven't been up the stables pinchin' that manure 'ave 'u." Said Sid with a grin?

"They guard that dung up there as if it were gold, Sid. 'u got a better chance of pinchin' coal."

"Aye 'u are right enough there Tom bach, takers that lot are not givers."

"I see 'u had an outin' with the top in your stall last week Sid," said Tom, "mind 'u, the top is pretty bad all round, I did mention it to Parfitt, but he didn't take much notice."

"I'm beginnin' to see the real Steve Parfitt, now Tom," said Sid, with a look of contempt upon his face. 'Not that nice guy who spoke to us on the first day outside the mine anymore is he? Just another bloody company man really when 'u get to know him, what do 'u say Tom?"

"I didn't expect nothing else Sid, 'u don't get those jobs for butterin' up to the men do 'u?"

As they were chatting Will Simmons came strolling down his garden path to join them, living next door to the Bishops as he did.

"I bet 'u two buggers are talkin' work even on your day off," he called out as he approached.

"No way," said Tom, "just comparin' your pathetic runner beans with ours, I'll give 'u a few tips if 'u like."

"What ar' 'u' talkin' about Tom, the other day I had to chase two sheep from under my cabbage leaves; and Dai James came into the garden and asked me if he could 'ave a swede or two, and I 'ad to tell 'im, those are not swedes Dai bach, they're radishes."

The gardening banter went on in the same humorous tone among friends but the topic soon got around to work, as Will had earlier alluded.

"U wouldn't think we lived next door to each other, Tom bach," said Will. "I 'aven't seen 'u for ages, but that's it, time we get 'ome and bathed there's no time for social callin'. Anyway while 'u're both 'ere now, how's it going at the level, I 'eard there's a bit of trouble with the top, is that right?"

"Aye, now me and Sid were just talkin' about it Will. Shaley old stuff 'u know, breaks off without warnin'. It's not a post and lid top, oh no, 'u got to put flats up all the time to make sure 'u cover the face. What really bothers me though is that the Main is also losing top between the laggin', now I've never seen that before. I've always had great respect for the work of 'ard-'eading boys up to now, but whoever drove the Pentrebach Main in, didn't 'ave that special skill. I looked at a few of their pairs of timber and 'u can see right through most of the joints, very poor notchin'; old Dan Cooper of the Holy-bush would turn in his grave."

"Pretty wet there too, I'm told," said Will. "Mind 'u we got the same problem at the Old Ivy, water runnin' down your back all day; we're bloody soaking comin' 'ome and it's a long walk down that mountain."

"Aye, it's wet in Pentrebach, alright," chirped in Sid. "But the coal itself is so dry that the air is still full of dust; so we got the worst of both worlds and with 'avin' to watch the top all the time, I must confess and I'm sure Tom'll agree, that the only thing we gained by switchin' is that the mine is much closer to home."

"Aye, 'u're right enough Sid, but we're there now and we're stuck with it," confessed Tom.

As they went on chatting Ben Bishop came strolling down Sid Llewellyn's garden path, he had just left his girlfriend Mabel Llewellyn at her house, having been out walking together.

"'Ave 'u set the date yet Ben?" Will called out as Ben approached.

"What date would that be now then Will?"

"Well u're weddin' date of course boy, time 'u made an 'onest woman of her now in'it and took some pressure of poor old Sid 'ere."

"Tell 'u what Will, if 'u'll pay for the weddin' I'll pop the question tomorrow." Ben responded humorously.

"With all the money these two buggers are makin' in that new mine, Duw 'elp, that should be nothin' to 'em mun."

All three collectively grinned at this last remark.

The sun was disappearing behind the wood-covered peak of the mountain, its last piercing rays making the leaves of the trees appear gossamer-like, their translucency exaggerated for just a brief moment. The four friends had parted and were making their ways to their respective doors; they would not be-long to their beds; an early start and another arduous day's work to face tomorrow.

7

A few weeks later Ben Bishop noticed something he had not seen before.

"Dad, did 'u see what Parfitt was carryin' earlier, a canary in a wire box and he 'ad the general manager with him, perhaps Will Simmons was right after all?"

"No, no Ben, it's nothin' to do with what Will Simmons said boy, they 'ave to check for gas every so often, it's standard practice. Now get a couple of posts and we'll put a flat up under that space b'there and stop worryin' about gas and canaries."

However, at that very moment Steve Parfitt was in debate on the subject of the 'spot check' findings, with the Colliery General Manager, Leslie Eaton, who had called at the Overman's request of a few days earlier concerning what the Overman described as an unusual smell he had noticed in the mine. The two men had been underground to investigate and were now standing just a few yards inside the mine.

"Well Mr Eaton, what do 'u make of it?"

"I don't rightly know Steve. What I find odd about it is that the smell appears more distinct in the Main. From that I would suggest that it's probably no more than pockets of foul air lingering above the lagging, which is why it's hardly noticeable lower down the mine and I found no trace of firedamp down there either.

"After inspecting the lagging Steve, we both noticed gaps above, which appear to travel some way up, indicating a disturbed strata and it is up there that the foul air and small traces of gas might have gathered. The safety lamp flame did rise a little but nothing serious. I'll bring the matter to the attention of Mr Driscoll our Mining Engineer and see what he makes of it. I wouldn't discuss it with the men for the moment though Steve, we don't want them jumping to the wrong conclusions."

"Of course not Mr Eaton, I'll wait 'til 'u come back to me and in the meantime just keep a quiet eye on it."

"Very well Steve, but I really don't think it's anything to bother about."

A couple of weeks later Leslie Eaton and Peter Driscoll were at Pentrebach Level, amid all sorts of conjecture on the part of the workers. After they had accompanied the Overman on a walkabout throughout the mine, taking safety lamps with them but no canary, they spent an hour or so in the site office.

Their conclusions, which they discussed with the Overman, agreed with what Mr Eaton had suggested earlier; that there were small deposits of foul air lingering above the lagging in the Main. However, if there was any firedamp in the mixture it was too limited to be of any significance.

"No significant change in the safety lamp flame," Mr Driscoll confirmed. "The foul air is giving off a bit of a smell but nothing to bother about, Leslie. We are hoping to begin work on a return airway or possibly an airshaft at the earliest opportunity, which will eliminate the problem. I don't want this business to be blown out of all proportion, Steve," he said, addressing the Overman directly. "So I would suggest you tell the workmen that the spot check revealed nothing of concern. As for the gaps above the lagging, perhaps you can get the Repairer to insert a few more slats across the disturbed areas as added support."

"Of course Mr Driscoll, I'll tell the men that both 'u and the manager inspected the mine and are satisfied that there is nothin' to worry about. I'll also tell them that work on the Return Airway or a shaft should begin soon."

"Yes, that ought to keep things in perspective Steve." Mr Driscoll agreed.

The following day Steve Parfitt spoke to the colliers as they gathered outside before the shift began.

"Right boys, five minutes of 'u're time before 'u go under; I know 'u're all wonderin' what the General Manager and the Engineer were doing 'ere yesterday. I 'ad reported traces of an unusual smell 'ere and there in the mine and wanted to get the matter looked into by management; just to be on the safe side like. Anyway, both Mr Eaton and Mr Driscoll, after investigatin' the area, believe it to be no more than a little foul air lingerin' in pockets where the fan takes longer to clear. They assured me that as soon as a return airway or airshaft is done, work on one or the other which is to begin soon, this will pass. And that's it lads, nothin' to worry about, so let's get this shift started now then is it?"

From then on no one - except perhaps secretly, Ben Bishop, who could not dismiss Will Simmons' earlier reference to gas from his mind - seemed to give the matter any further thought. As a matter of fact there was a more pressing problem worrying the colliers than the off chance of a little gas. The top was getting progressively more splintered as the coalface moved forward; the men having to increase their timbering and leave broader pillars, not something the Overman or indeed the men were very pleased about, as it reduced the pace of output

The Overman was making a modest allowance for the extra time taken to secure the top but it, nevertheless, put a lot more strain on the colliers psychologically. One man had received a serious injury to his hand when a large piece of shale had suddenly slipped from between the posts and severed his wrist. As a result he was unable to move his fingers and was not expected to return to work for a long time, if at all.

Just a few days later, Tom and Ben Bishop were working in their stall when, about mid-shift, they heard a loud thud and Sid Llewellyn in the next stall, screaming out for help. Rushing to his aid the Bishops found that a fall had occurred and while Sid was unhurt there was no sign of his helper, young Clive Baker.

"God help me Tom, I think I've lost the boy," Sid blurted out in a state of obvious distress and panic.

"'old on now Sid, let's see what we're up against," cried Tom, though he could see quite clearly that the fall was serious, before them was a pile of debris reaching almost to the top of the stall.

The three men, soon to be helped by all the other colliers who had heard the commotion, began frantically digging to remove the mass of stone and shale before them, which had engulfed the stall and, undoubtedly the poor young lad. While they worked they kept calling the boy's name but, alas, there was no response.

It wasn't long before Steve Parfitt, the two shotsmen and the two alliers arrived. As soon as the Overman was made aware of the seriousness of the situation, he sent a message back to the surface to send someone to get in touch with the General Manager. Somehow, by the time news of the fall had got about it was believed that a number of men were buried beneath it and this encouraged the setting off of the hooter. By a strange twist of fate it was Dewi Baker, the steam haulage operator and father of Clive Baker, who set the hooter in motion.

With all hands frantically working it didn't take too long to recover the body of fifteen year old Clive Baker.

However, when the futility of their efforts became a reality, poor old Sid Llewellyn was so overcome that he just sat there with his head in his hands crying like a baby.

The boy's badly mutilated body was carried out on a stretcher completely covered in a collection of heavy coats.

Steve Parfitt was annoyed that the surface men had sounded the hooter, concerned that it will have alarmed the whole village and caused an unnecessary panic. However, when he heard that Dewi Baker was responsible he kept his composure and decided not to raise the matter. As the poor lad's body was brought out of the mine the surface workers gathered around to learn whose it was; including Dewi Baker; his boy's name having been already mentioned.

"Let me see 'im," he demanded, "let me see 'im."

"No Dewi," the Overman intervened. "You best not Dewi, let's get 'im down to the village and into a safe place, Dewi bach." He pleaded.

But the distraught father had already pushed his way to the stretcher where the boy lay and pulled some garments back to reveal his face. The shock of the sight of the boy's unrecognisable features was too much for the tragic man and he shouted:

"That's not my boy! 'u've got it wrong, that's not my Clive! That's not my Clive, 'u've made a terrible mistake. Where is my boy? Where is my Clive?"

The men, including Sid Llewellyn, who was still in a confused state of trauma and shock, tried desperately to comfort the grieving father.

From that time on not a word was spoken as they began to carry the dead boy down the mountainside, his father having to be supported and comforted as they moved on. They hadn't gone very far, however, when they espied a large group of people ascending from the village who - responding to the hooter - had made their way up to the mine. They had at first been delayed by the vicar who suggested that they should let the colliers deal with the immediate situation, whatever it may be, "In case we get in the way." But patience was short and the villagers had soon set forth in earnest. Seeing them approach, the overman rushed on to meet them and explain the situation, after which the whole gathering of workers and villagers continued the descent in melancholy silence.

Later Leslie Eaton and Steve Parfitt accompanied by Peter Driscoll and the two Deputies returned to the mine to inspect the scene of the accident and take details, which would be needed at the later inevitable Official Inquiry.

The funeral of young Clive Baker raised a cloud of grief over the entire village of Pentrebach. The mine was closed for a few days while the incident was investigated and was to remain closed until the funeral had taken place. Squire Watkins had sent a message, informing the Baker family that regrettably, he would not be able to attend the funeral due to a business commitment he was unable to avoid; instead his bailiff attended with a large wreath and a letter of condolence. This cold and distant attitude was not uncommon with those of his society. The message concluded with a promise that he, through the owners and management, will ensure the tragic circumstances are thoroughly investigated.

After the young lad's corpse was prepared for burial *ddewiddu (*finishing) for the next few nights some volunteer neighbours sat up in the room with the coffin, out of respect; a tradition known as *gwylio'r corf* (watching the dead).

However, with a break in tradition Clive Baker's four sisters accompanied by their father and mother, walked slowly behind the horse-drawn hearse all the way to Capel Pentre graveyard. Customarily women did not attend the cortège but preceded it to the church, there to await the arrival of the hearse and the men, who would have walked in slow procession behind it. Older women would have remained at the home of the deceased to prepare a meal upon the return of relatives and near friends. However, given the great tragedy, on this occasion the girls and Mrs Baker had been allowed to join the male mourners.

The vicar expressed the tragic loss of one so young and the ever present dangers of his occupation.

"We live," he said, "ever aware of the hazards of mining, but in a mining community like ours the fire in the hearth and food upon the table, are wholly dependent upon those who must work beneath the ground.

"To the Baker family we offer our prayers and sincere condolences; let them turn to the Lord for guidance as they face this tragedy which, neither we nor they can understand and find so hard to bear. In the lord we must trust and believe that our questions will be answered come the day of judgement."

Clive Baker was buried in his paternal grand-parents grave.

Due to his age and the suddenness of Clive Baker's death it was appreciated that his family were ill-prepared to meet the cost of the funeral and funeral feast. In keeping with tradition, therefore, at the end of the funeral service a gentleman, conspicuous by his location, who had been selected as the chief mourner, left his pew and placed a silver coin on the communion table; the rest of the mourners followed his example, making similar donations or what they could afford. In most cases this money would be for the clergyman's services. But in situations like this, the vicar being aware of the family's unfortunate circumstances, would divide the collection equally between himself and the family of the deceased.

The investigation into the cause of Clive Baker's death found no fault with the state of the stall and was satisfied that his collier, Sid Llewellyn, had followed all procedures common to his duty. It would appear that the fall was the result of an 'abnormally disturbed top,' the collapse of which could not have been anticipated. The investigators, therefore, were entirely satisfied that the boy's death was the result of nothing more than a tragic accident

At a later Inquest, Clive Baker's death was, based upon the evidence put forward, again declared entirely accidental. The Coroner, in view of the circumstances, therefore, concluded that "tragic and unfortunate as this accident was, any further enquiry would be very unlikely to determine an alternative outcome."

Sid Llewellyn did return to work but requested that he work with another collier from then on, feeling unable to accept the responsibility of a second boy in his charge. His request was granted.

Dewi Baker took some time to return to his job at the winding house but needs must and he was welcomed back by all the men with compassion and understanding; though he was constantly haunted by the thought of ever having to operate the hooter again.

Whenever there was a fatal accident in a colliery it took a little time for things to get back to normal, especially so in the place where the accident occurred. Sid Llewellyn never did return to the stall where young Clive Baker was killed. It was agreed that he would take a new stall and that Michael Donovan, one of the Irish men from Riverside Row, would work with him.

Sid's stall was taken over by Andrew Lloyd and his fourteen year old son Fred who had recently moved to Pentrebach, looking for work. Andrew's other boy, twelve year old Hugh, was also given a start and would work alongside his father and brother as a trainee. Andrew and Fred were made aware of the accident but as they were unfamiliar with the boy they were content to take the stall on. While they expressed their sorrow at the young lad's tragic death, they felt that as they had just moved into the village and Clive Baker was no more than a name to them, it could not have the impact upon them that it must have had on his family and those who knew him.

8

Some weeks after the sad Baker boy incident, the coalface began to narrow down to less than one foot of coal. A Fault had occurred where the strata, as a result of an early geological disturbance, had been squeezed and pressed and this had caused the coal seam to drift to the right, resulting in a change of direction for the Pentrebach mine. For some time the colliers were to witness a number of strange faces on the scene. One, apparently, was a geologist and others were leading figures in the coalmining industry. Of course Lesley Eaton and Peter Driscoll were also present.

The geologist described the fault as a balk fault, caused by a sudden depression in the top of the coal seam which reduced the seam considerably - more prevalent where the top is shale, as in this instance. In this case the seam had been flattened almost to the 'thill' or bottom of the seam.

While the coal face did gradually rise again and return to normal, they had been forced to follow the much reduced seam for quite some distance over a period of several weeks, when very little coal was produced and they were now progressing to the right of the original seam. However, there was some good news the loose shaley features had gone and in its place a more or less sound top.

While things were considerably easier and safer for the colliers since the top had improved, the air- perhaps due to the diversion- seemed to be getting progressively heavier near the coal face. This may have arisen as a result of the fan becoming less effective after the change in direction. Whatever, it made for warmer conditions causing the men to sweat heavily and experience some breathing difficulties when over exerting. The men showed their concern by approaching Steve Parfitt before starting a shift one morning. They wanted some pressure put on the management to hasten the cutting of the return airway or shaft. They gathered around the Overman at the mouth of the mine.

"As I told 'u boys," the Overman repeated, "work on the return airway is to start soon. I understand that they are waitin' for the 'ard-'eading boys, who've been tied up with a big job in a mine in the other valley. Failin' this they may go for a shaft instead. I'm sure you'll agree that there's not much they can do 'til these boys are available, now is there?"

But the men were not happy with this half promise and asked the Overman to bring the matter to the attention of Mr Eaton once again.

"Tell 'im that if somethin' isn't done soon we won't be able to work 'ere Steve." Tom Bishop exclaimed. "u can take my word for it Steve, if anythin' will push um into action it's a threat to production."

"O K boys I'll get onto 'im this afternoon and point out the difficulties 'u're 'aving in the face. Now let's get this shift started or there'll be no coal out today and that won't go down well will it now?"

"Don't u' go lettin' us down now Steve," shouted Michael Donovan, "it's gettin' bloody uncomfortable down there, to be sure it is."

With that, all the men bellowed their agreement convincing the Overman that something needed be done and pretty soon at that.

Sam Thorn was the Repairer, whose job it was to tend to the general maintenance of the dram road and supports in the Main, should they need any attention, and to couple the drams and shackle the journey to the haulage rope before signalling the winding house to pull them up the drift. The Overman had indicated to him that Mr Driscoll had left orders that he should increase the cross-slats in the Main where he could see noticeable gaps, though he had not yet got round to it being busy with other things. He too had complained to the Overman of 'the smell hangin' about the drift like.' The overman, simply repeating his now standard response, that it was no more than pockets of foul air and not a problem, content in the knowledge that both the Engineer and General Manager had dismissed the matter without concern.

Soon Christmas 1862 arrived with still no sign of any work on any form of airway. Despite just a two day break, Christmas Day and Boxing Day, The Bishops were determined to have a merry time and to help this along, Gwladys had warned Tom and Ben that there was to be no talk of work; so the air and the airways at the mine were not up for debate.

By now the whole village was warming to the festive season. The Pentrebach Inn was, of course, full of men enjoying a drink without the pressure of getting up the next morning. Equally full were Bethel Chapel and Capel Pentre, for at that time religion still played a significant part in the festivities; unlike the commercial Christmases of later years. Very few failed to attend either chapel or church and that included most of the miners.

The only school in the village other than the Sunday school, held at Capel Pentre, had been Miss Weaver's Dame School. This had been no more than a nursery as no child over the age of ten would be sent there. Sadly, Miss Weaver, who had been a popular figure, though her teaching was primarily based upon the bible, good behaviour and manners, passed away in October 1861. So the onus to bring the little ones together for a Christmas concert had fallen on Bethel Chapel. There was talk, however, of a National School soon to be raised in the village, which would be government supported. Nonetheless, as boys could still start work underground from as early twelve years of age, even the 'new' school would only cater for the very young.

The Bishops were up early on Christmas morning. Dressing up in their Sunday best they left the house to join many others making their way to Capel Pentre to attend the 6 a.m. Plygain service. Pentrebach was among a number of villages still observing this tradition. It was customary for everyone to bring a candle along and if the weather was fair –hardly any wind- they would light them before entering the church. The church would be decked with many more candles often of different colours. Ben Bishop had separated himself from his parents and sister to walk ahead with Mabel Llewellyn, the courting couple making the most of the opportunity. The vicar conducted the service, when he touched upon gratitude for those traditional needs: food on the table and fire in the hearth; the joy of good health and love of children. He also offered a special blessing to the Baker family for the recent sad loss of their boy, Clive.

Goose was the traditional Christmas fare and the Bishops had a very large one as the Llewellyns, consisting of Sid, his wife Susan and their daughter Mabel were to join the Bishops this year, last year it had been the other way round. In the evening Tom and Sid went off to the Pentrebach Inn for a few beers – though under orders not to be too late - while Gwladys, May and Susan relaxed with a cup of tea and a chat in the back kitchen, allowing Ben and Mabel to occupy the living room for an hour or so, that they could be on their own.

The two men, dutifully, got home in reasonable time and both families enjoyed a couple of glasses of sherry and a cheerful get-together, where everyone took part in a few hours' friendly conversation, in between which Mabel, who often sang solo at Capel Pentre and had done so at that morning's Plygain service, give a delightful rendition of some popular carols. At the end of the night they all joined in the final and favourite carol – Silent Night.

As they moved into the New Year and the month of January, the quality of the air became the number one topic at the mine. On the morning of the 14th January the men had unanimously agreed not to go underground until they had once more spoken to Steve Parfitt about it. They were now determined to get something done and if need be, refuse to work until it was. Tom Bishop was their appointed spokesman so he approached the Overman at the mouth of the mine.

"Somethin' 'as got to be done about the air Steve," Tom stressed. "What 'as 'appened to any of the airway projects which was supposed to 'ave started long before Christmas?"

"The last time I spoke to Mr Eaton about it," the Overman declared, "he informed me that the makin' of one or other of the airways is definitely to start sometime in February; I was goin' to announce it this comin' week end."

"Even if they do start work on an airway by then, and I'm not convinced," said Tom, "it's goin' to take a long time to complete; we want somethin' done about the air now Steve, not in a couple of months' time. What about another or bigger fan? Get on to Eaton and Driscoll today Steve, or 'u may find us downing tools 'ere."

This was a direct threat which took the Overman by surprise. To so much as suggest strike action would be taken as an affront to the company's authority and the response from the management would be harsh and uncompromising. But the Overman could detect the determination in the eyes of all those present, so he decided not to make matters worse by being too high handed.

"Now steady on Tom bach. First of all I don't 'ave the authority to contact Mr Driscoll direct but I will get in touch with Mr Eaton today, I'll make a special journey down to see him; that's the best I can do Tom"

Tom moved back to where the men were assembled to report on Parfitt's response. After a little while he called the Overman to join them addressing him bluntly.

"Right Steve," he began, "we've unanimously decided that unless somethin' is done about the air by the end of the week, or someone in authority 'as assured us that it will be, we will not turn up for work on Monday next.

"I don't know what's come over 'u Tom but I think 'u and the men better be careful how far 'u go; or 'u could all find 'u'rselves out of a job by next week."

With that the Overman hurriedly left the scene.

The men, in an obvious mood of discontent, made their way into the mine to begin their shift. On the way in they met Sam Thorn who was curious as to why they were so late coming in. He was attending to two loose dram rails which had separated creating a gap between them, which needed to be closed before any coal could be taken out.

"Where 'ave 'u been then boys and where's Parfitt, not like 'im to be late, the Shotsmen and Alliars 'ave gone in?"

Tom stopped to explain the situation to the Repairer who confirmed that he too had reported foul air to Parfitt, some time ago.

"If 'u boys down tools I'll join 'u," Sam declared, "It's time they did somethin' at the very least a stronger fan although at the moment Tom, it don't make much difference that 'u are late 'u wouldn't be able to get any coal out just yet, I got a bloody big gap in the road to sort out."

"We'd give 'u a 'and Sam, only we got quite a bit of catchin' up to do like."

"Not to worry Tom bach, I'll get it sorted."

With that the men made their way to the coalface and Sam got on with his job.

9

It took Sam the Repairer some time to re-join the two rails that had parted on one side of the dram road, but if truth be told it was not a job well done. Two sections of the rail should have been raised and re-aligned in order to be sure that they were brought to a close properly and that the level of the joints was flush. However, that would have taken a long time and was not really a one man job. Sam instead, decided to simply use a crow bar to gradually lever the rail supports on either side of the gap and thereby bring the rails together; tightening the road spikes as an extra precaution; not something he hadn't done before. He was determined not to further delay the first journey, the colliers already having lost enough time as a result of the meeting with the Overman.

By the time Sam got back to the double parting the sixth dram, making a full journey, was just arriving. The Alliar, Ivor Williams, released the dram from the cob and then he and Sam pushed it close enough to couple it to the fifth dram. Sam checked the couplings of each of the six drams in turn and attached the bar-hook at the rear and then the haulage rope to the first dram ready for withdrawal.

"Everything oright Ivor?" asked Sam. 'I've just finished fixin' a gap in the rails, bugger of a job it was too mind 'u."

"Aye, the lads are coalin' well, despite the poor air Sam," said Ivor, "but Parfitt 'ad better come up with some answers soon or the way the lads are talkin', there'll be no work next week."

"Well, let's get this first journey out then," Sam declared. "There 'ave been enough 'oldups this mornin' as it is."

With that Sam pulls sharply on the galvanised signal wire running on smooth small circular china discs attached to the posts on the side of the road. Three sharp pulls resulted in the spring-bell in the engine house corresponding with three rings; the signal for the haulage man to begin hauling the journey out.

The drams move off and begin gathering speed as the two men watch. They carry on debating the air problem and what each of them think might happen when the Overman presents the colliers' grievances to the General Manager.

"I don't think Eaton or Driscoll are going to be very 'appy about it," said Sam. "They don't like anyone threatenin' to down tools."

"That's true enough Sam bach," said Ivor, "but it's they who are at fault not the men; that airway should 'ave been cut a long time ago."

Suddenly their debate was interrupted by what sounded like a roll of thunder followed by a mighty thud which was itself succeeded by a brisk rush of air.

The two men were totally unaware that as the journey reached the point where Sam had re-joined the rails, the first three drams passed over without any trouble but the fourth dram reopened the gap. The rear wheel meeting the resistance of the iron rails within the gap, yet still spinning at speed had created a fountain of sparks flying in all directions. Thus a small pocket of gas, concealed high above the spot, was ignited and simultaneously a series of similar small pockets of gas, which had been holding undetected well over the loose rooftop slats, were also ignited. The effect was to create a running ball of fire leading to a massive explosion bringing the none-too secure top crashing down, from the location of the gap in the rail to the mouth of the mine, a distance of near thirty yards or more; the mine was thereby effectively sealed off.

This kind of explosion with a running ball of fire is usually followed by the effects of an after damp; where the gas creates a mix of poisonous carbon monoxide fumes which could well have killed the miners instantly. However, in this instance the ball of fire run towards the mouth of the mine and was thereby expelled via the portal into the atmosphere.

For a moment the two men stood still, a little dazed by the suddenness of the blast.

"What the 'ell was that?" Sam cried.

"Sounds like an explosion to me," said Ivor. "Are 'u oright Sam?"

"Aye I'm oright Ivor, we'd better go and see what's 'appened."

The incline being quite steep and with poor lighting, their progress up the drift was very slow. After a time, however, they arrived at the place where Sam had been working and were surprised to see just two stationary drams. Beyond this was a wall of rock reaching to the top of the road. They knew instantly that there was no immediate way out and that they and all the other men were effectively trapped.

They moved up to the two drams to examine them and could then see half of the third dram, the remainder lying under the fall. They discovered that the rear wheel of the third dram, closest to them, was wedged between the re-opened gap.

"This is where I was workin' Ivor," declared Sam. "The rails must have parted again, this might have brought the journey to a standstill but what caused the explosion?"

"The only thing that could cause an explosion in 'ere Sam," said Ivor, "is gas, and the only thing that could cause gas to explode is a spark. My guess is that the this dram wheel -pointing to the third dram half exposed- wedged as it is between the rails, kept spinnin' causing some sparks which lit the gas; quite a lot of it by the looks of things Sam bach."

They were not to know just how accurate his observations were.

As they stood there deliberating the cause and effect of the explosion and staring at the now completely sealed off roadway, they heard some movement behind them. Turning round they could see a string of moving lights ascending the drift, all the other men and boys, having heard the explosion and felt the blast of air throughout the mine, were trudging up the drift towards them to determine what had happened.

Within a short time the entire workforce of twenty-one men and four boys were all staring at the mass of rock and rubble which had fallen and barred their only way out. Eddie Jones and Clive Harding pushed their way to the front; as appointed Deputies they would be expected to take charge.

Clive Harding was an Englishman who had moved to Wales some years earlier. Having had a reasonable standard of education he had soon qualified as a Deputy/Shotsman; a good natured man he was quite popular among his colleagues.

The two men began by inspecting the two and a half visible drams. The gap into which the wheel of the third dram had lodged was clear to see, and both men determined that there must have been a loose couple of road spikes at that point and the sudden weight and speed of the journey had forced the joining rails apart. They called Sam over for his opinion on their findings.

Sam was left with no choice but to explain his actions of the day, as others were already aware of his attempts to deal with the gap.

"Jesus, Sam, that's not a job you should have taken on, on your own; it's obvious that you left a weak joint." Clive Harding raged.

"Listen 'ere now Clive, it's not that unusual for joints to open or drams to come off the road for that matter and I've often 'ad to do the repairin' on my own, so don't 'u go blaming me for this bloody explosion." Sam declared, in much the same tone.

"'old on now boys," Tom Bishop interrupted. "Surely the most important thing at the moment is to figure out how the 'ell we are goin' to get out of 'ere, whether it's any body's fault or not won't make much bloody difference if we can't."

The reminder of the awareness of their predicament did, indeed, bring any further debate on the cause and who -if anyone- was to blame, to an end.

"Tom is right," said Eddy Jones, "we need to assess the degree of the blockage and to see if we can make any contact with the surface."

"Of course," said Harding, "and I'm sorry for jumping down your throat Sam, no one is pointing the finger of blame at you; you did what you thought was best and you could not have possibly known what was going to happen.

With that he took the situation in hand, declaring:

"I agree with you lads we need to investigate properly and see what we can do; besides we may only be a few yards from the other side of the fall. Let's pitch in and see how much we can move; don't forget they will be aware of the situation outside and will have organised a proper dig from that end by now. I would suggest, due to the limited room and not to tire ourselves out too quickly, that two men work either side of the journey in fifteen minute intervals. But first of all a few volunteers to go and get some tools lads, from the coalface."

With that several men left to attend to this errand.

"Before they come back," Harding continued. "I would like to see if we can determine whether the air and water pipes have been completely flattened under the fall. I must, therefore, ask you all to be quiet for a minute while I listen for any movement within the pipes."

With that he bent down and put his ear to one and then the other of the pipes.

"No, I'm afraid I can't hear any movement in either of the pipes but I will try tapping them to see if we get any response from outside; everybody quiet now."

However, before the deputy began to tap the pipes, the silence itself creating an eerie atmosphere, the youngest of the boys began to cry and scream out:-

"Are we goin' to die? Are we goin' to die?"

"Someone take him back out of the way lads will you." Harding whispered, fully understanding the poor boy's reaction, after all he was only twelve years old.

The boy was Hugh Lloyd the little trainee and it was his father Andrew who, putting his arm around the lad's shoulders, led him away from the area to comfort him.

"Come on lad, let the boys see what they do; I'm sure they'll work somethin' out."

Harding began tapping the pipes with a piece of stone and pausing between every four or five taps to listen for any response. The silence between the tapping was intense, but alas, the only sound was that of the heavy collective breathing of the miners. There was no response from outside.

"Listen now boys we mustn't be put off by this" said Harding. "Maybe the only reason we got no response is because the pipes are flattened and no sound can travel either way."

Soon the men came back with the tools and work began, using the method of two either side of the journey as proposed by Harding. It wasn't long, however, before they realised what a hopeless task they were confronted with. Immediately to the sides of the exposed drams were some large lose boulders and these, after several changes of men, they managed to break up and move. However, at this point they were confronted by a sheer rock face and with only shovels, mandrels and sledgehammers, with all the will and effort in the world, even after several hours, they made very little impression upon this solid wall.

It wasn't just the heat and exhaustion and sheer muscular fatigue, that was beginning to seriously affect the men, the ever-present knowledge of their predicament was having a huge psychologically damaging toll upon them; especially the younger lads. It was Harding who tried to boost their morale by telling them that he was sure they will have made considerable progress from the outside by now and that he was convinced it would not be long before there will be audible evidence of this.

These words of attempted comfort, however, had little effect upon the younger men and boys. So dejected were they by now that they lacked the spirit to go on battling against such overwhelming odds.

Eventually, it was agreed to suspend all further efforts to break the rocks, it was just not physically possible to make any positive progress and such futile endeavour only consumed valuable oxygen quicker and unnecessarily weakened those exerting themselves. It was agreed, therefore, to get as comfortable as possible and sit or lie listening for any activity without.

10

Earlier Harding had got the men to place all the food and water they had in a chosen spot in order to assess their supply that he may organise a system of rationing. Fortunately, the explosion had occurred before their meal break, so no one had eaten and all lunch-boxes and water jacks were still full. He'd also taken charge of the lighting. After the cessation of their attempt to break the rock he suggested that just two tallow candles be kept alight for comfort sake and that he alone would keep his oil-wick cap light burning, as he intended to write some notes in his Shotsman's duty book by way of a record of the events leading up to and after the explosion. He concluded by asking the men if they were all happy to agree with his suggestions. There was a general murmur of approval though most were now just too tired, despondent and disconsolate to care.

It had been decided that the four cobs, now all brought back from the working area to a little way above the double parting, should be tethered with sufficient room for them to eat from their nose bags and lie down; there was nothing else they could do for them.

"Has anyone besides me got a watch?" asked Harding.

"Yes, I've got one." Sam the Repairer replied. "I always carry one to keep pace with the journey times."

"Well let's check the time now to make sure we agree Sam."

This they did, when Harding told Sam that they should both keep track of the time and especially so "if we are to be 'ere for more than one day."

"I will mark the turning of one day into the next with a cross cut into this post," Harding indicated. "It would be very easy to lose track of the days under here with nothing to indicate change. I'm sure the water will keep at bay for quite some time and there will be sufficient air for just as long"

The younger boys were, nonetheless, getting frightened and kept asking how long it will be before the rescue team breaks through. Harding tried his best to offer periodic words of optimism:

"My guess is that it'll take another 'hour so at the most." But after several hours had past:-

"They're probably debating whether to use explosives to get in quicker." And so on.

As the time went slowly by the only thing that endured was silence; most passed into sporadic involuntary phases of sleep; but not Harding. He began to write notes. He had a leather container in which his Deputy/Shotsman's duty book was kept, in order to keep it dry and safe. He wasn't to know it then but he would be making daily entries in his note book for a few more days. Eventually, when his final entry was made, he would place the duty book inside its leather container and tear off some of his moleskin trousers from his lower leg, wind that around the container and hold it together with shot-wire. He would then place it in the inside pocket of his jacket in a last attempt to preserve it.

By the middle of the second day, with no evidence of any activity from without, a continued atmosphere of despondency hung heavily over all.

It was Andrew Lloyd who, in an attempt to engender some encouragement especially in the case of the younger lads, broke the silence when he addressed Harding.

"Are we really going to just sit 'ere and hope the recue team get to us, Clive? Seems to me we are not setting a very good example to the youngsters 'ere, adopting a totally defeatist stance. Why don't we 'ave another go at that rock; it could be that we're just a few yards from the end of the fall?"

"I understand where you're coming from Andrew but you know how little progress we were making and how exhausting our efforts were. I'm convinced that the rock now facing us is a total blank wall and that with no real tools to deal with it we will be using up our reserve energy and valuable breathing air, for nothing. But, if the lads want to have a go, it's fine by me," Harding responded.

"What do you say boys?" Andrew asked.

However, before anyone could respond Ken Jones, Wally Jones' son, called out.

"Clive! I thought 'u and Eddie was shotsmen. Well, 'u got powder and pills and firin' equipment 'an stuff, so why 'aven't 'u bored some holes in the rock and tried to blast our way out?"

Harding was well aware of the tension and near panic that by now was affecting, not just the youngsters, but everyone else. So he turned to the boy and explained.

"Ken, if we thought for one minute that we could blast our way out of here, I can assure you that both me and Eddie would have had a go at it by now. That you have had to ask before one of the older colliers mentioned it is something of a clue, Ken lad. To begin with it's very doubtful that our drill would penetrate the rock and I'm afraid Ken, the powder we use to fire the coal and the bottom and top holes would have little or no effect upon that solid wall of rock and of course these colliers know it; which is why they didn't bring the matter up. Besides which, we could cause another explosion if there are any more pockets of gas about. And the smoke from the firing, especially as there is so little movement in the air without the fan, would create an atmosphere that would make breathing even more difficult. I'm sorry, Ken lad, but it just wouldn't work."

The poor lad sat down next to his brother and father who, putting an arm around him, whispered:

"You were right to ask my boy but Clive is also right; we don't have nothin' that could hope to touch that rock. But they will have stronger stuff outside so don't 'u worry now lad."

With that Andrew Lloyd resumed his call for another go at the rock and a vote was cast.

A decision was reached to have one last attempt to break the rock and every man and boy -with the exception of the little trainee- took turns in this endeavour. Alas, after several hours of intensive labour, very little impression had been made on the seemingly impervious material. During this desperate but futile engagement a lot of drinking water had been consumed and the physically wearing effect upon the men was considerable. The sad thing was that not only had Andrew's suggestion proved futile, it had done more harm to the morale of the very youngsters he was hoping to inspire.

After it was agreed to suspend the work, Clive Harding pointed out that from now on they will have to be more sparing with the drinking water.

"I want you to know that I don't think there was anything wrong with Andrew's suggestion to have another go but I think you'll all agree that it just didn't come off. I'm afraid we really do have no choice but to pin our hopes on those better equipped lads on the outside. We must, nevertheless, not give up and keep listening for that breakthrough."

After the marking of the second cross on the post, Tom Bishop sat next to Clive Harding and the two men, between long periods of involuntary sleep, spoke in whispers to one another. Both men agreed that it was becoming less likely that they will be rescued in time; not a sound had emitted from the direction of the fall, clear evidence that the extent of the fall was considerable.

"Judging by the lack of any activity from beyond the fall Tom,' said Harding. "It looks likely that we really are up against a solid mass, if this is the case and it extends to the mouth, there is no way they will be able to get through to us; I fear we may be lost, my friend."

"We can only 'ope Clive bach," Tom declared, in a sombre melancholy tone. "It's the young ones I feel most sorry for tho' Clive, like my boy 'ere (who was lying alongside him seemingly fast asleep) with all to live for and those with young families waitin' outside"

"Yes Tom, that sad little twelve year-old and the others like your son; just starting their lives, poor souls and as you say the others, the three Irish lads for instance, with young families out there. It's so sad that the Return Airway has not been cut Tom, there's every chance we could have all walked out of here unharmed."

"It's all about money Clive, money is God. The irony of it is that it's unlikely that they will ever make another penny from this mine."

"Do 'u think that Fault we had to overcome, that changed the direction of the mine, helped bring about a further delay in the cuttin' of the Return Airway, Clive?" Tom asked.

"Definitely Tom," Clive replied. "It took several weeks to bypass it, so they would not have been happy to be losing coaling time so early in the life of the mine. Although they were lucky it was such a limited barrier, just a narrowing of the coalface which made us veer to the right for a distance before we could pick up the proper seam again. Generally, when a mine hits a Fault it's lost altogether. Yes, there's no doubt Tom that after the Fault, cutting a Return Airway was not an immediate priority. But that's business Tom and our employers are, if nothing else, business people and these practices are not uncommon among all other coal owners, it's just the way things are Tom."

Ben Bishop woke with a start, for a moment not realising where he was. When all came back to him he nudged his father and asked what is happening.

"There is nothin' more we can do from this end now Ben bach. We are listenin' for any activity from the outside. I'm sure we won't have to wait too long my boy."

"It looks like Will Simmons had a point after all dad, didn't he?" Ben suddenly declared.

"Nobody could have predicted this Ben, least of all Will Simmons. But don't 'u lose 'eart my boy, they'll get us out."

But even as he spoke, he knew his son was too experienced to be fooled and must surely harbour the same doubts as Harding and himself.

"It's no good pretendin' dad; I know things are looking bad. It's just the thought of not seeing Mam or May or my lovely Mabel ever again. I wonder what they are thinkin' out there now dad, waitin' and worryin' about us. I wish I could send them a message. I'd tell Mabel how much I love her and tell mam and May how much I'm thinkin' of 'um and long to be with 'um.

"I don't know how to die dad; I just keep bursting into tears every few minutes."

"Believe me my boy, none of us 'ere are 'eroes, you only find them in story books, we are just victims of circumstances beyond our control; each of us dealin' with it in his own way. I can assure 'u that u're no less brave than the next man my boy. But don't 'u go givin' up 'ope just yet Ben bach."

With that Sid Llewellyn who was sitting nearby turned to Ben.

"I just want 'u to know Ben bach, how much we are 'oping 'u will become our son-in-law, I realise things are looking bad at the moment my boy, but there is still a chance that they'll break through. And believe me Ben bach, none of us knows how to die; as your father said, all those stories of 'eroes facing death with super courage are exactly that, stories; found in fiction."

By the time Clive Harding had cut the third cross on the post, and the food and water rations were running seriously low, it wasn't just him, Tom Bishop and Ben who were convinced that there was not going to be a rescue team after all. Thankfully however, for most of the time the men and boys slept, the air now being so heavy and warm sleeping came all too readily.

On the beginning of the fourth day Clive Harding asked Tom Bishop if he felt up to coming with him to see how far the water had advanced. For a moment it took a considerable effort on the part of both men, their bodies having difficulty in responding to their demands, just to stand up. This achieved, they struggled down the mine clutching at the posts for support as they did. With little vision, their oil-wick lamps affording poor lighting; having left the remaining two tallow candles with the others, every step was a challenge.

On their way they passed the four cobs each tethered to a post. There was nothing they could do for them and to set them free would be foolish, in that they would not be able to control them and they could even injure or kill one or other of the now very weak men. It wasn't long beyond the cobs before they reached the double parting and then the water level, which meant that the entire work area was already completely submerged. They scooped some water up in the two jacks they had brought with them; while they would not, under normal circumstances ever resort to drinking this water, if the need became too great, there may be no choice. Viewing their predicament from where they stood they were well aware that with no sign of any rescue team, there was very little room or time for optimism.

When they returned those awake were eager to learn how far the water had advanced and both Harding and Bishop had already decided to tell them exactly what they had found; there was little point in hiding the truth at this stage. However, they still tried to encourage everyone to go on listening for any signs of a rescue attempt. But the younger lads were by now in such absolute despair that they turned away and one shouted at Harding and Bishop to shut-up and stop pretending that there is any chance of getting out. Neither man responded, appreciating that it was unfair to try to instil false hope. There followed a very uneasy silence, save for some quiet sobbing.

After a while this silence was quite suddenly broken when three of young boys: Fred Lloyd and Ken and Brian Jones, showing an amazing and inexplicable burst of energy, each picked up a mandrel and raced towards the blockage where they began fiercely jabbing at the solid rock. This was a frenzied attack which resulted in sparks flying everywhere. Some of the men rushed towards them but in fear of being injured by the flailing mandrels, could only shout their protests in an attempt to restrain the desperate young lads' moment of madness.

It wasn't long, however, before the three totally drained youngsters, almost simultaneously; fell to the ground in tears and total despair.

"'u could have caused another explosion," shouted one of the miners, "an' blown us all to bits."

In response Ken Jones raised his head and turned to the speaker, his black face streaked by streaming tears.

"What the bloody 'ell do you think we was trying to do; better that than lying 'ere waitin' for death to creep up on us, i'n'it.?

There really was no answer to that and no one offered one.

Not long after this incident they felt a tremor and later a further two.

"They must be trying to dynamite their way in to reach us?" Someone shouted."

"Yes, I'm sure that's what it is, Harding replied, "there's still hope lads; there's still hope."

But this glimmer of hope was soon to founder as there followed a long silence, a clear indication that the would-be rescue team had abandoned all efforts.

As the day drew to a close there was a sudden loud high pitched gurgling sound as the poor cobs could be heard struggling to fight against the ever encroaching water. One of the young lads called out:

"The ponies are drowning! The ponies are drowning! We're next! We're next!" -His last few words not much above a whisper.

It was a heartrending but truthful declaration and it wasn't just the young lads who could be heard sobbing now.

Breathing was becoming in itself a task. Thankfully, for most, involuntary sleep was to develop into a kind of comatose-like relief as time moved on. But it was inevitably the young boys who were able to cope with the diminishing oxygen more easily and so it was they who were witnessing the laboured breathing of the older men, as life faded from their bodies.

All the oil-wick lights and tallow candles had long extinguished as the young eyes stared into the void of absolute darkness. There is nothing as blank as the darkness of a mine. It challenges the imagination, which will try to invent a vision of comfort. One young croaking voice could be heard calling "Mam, mam, where ar 'u mam." It was twelve year old Hugh Lloyd.

Hugh was lying close to his brother Fred, as they attempted to offer each other some degree of comfort. Suddenly they heard a squeaking sound and the rapid movement of something rushing over the ground.

"What's that noise?" whispered Hugh into Fred's ear.

"I think it's the rats Hugh, comin' out of their 'oles because of the water."

And this is exactly what it was. Up to now the rats, which were common place in the mines where ponies were used –brought in via the ponies' feed sacks- had for the most part remained hidden, although they could occasionally be seen scampering about. Now, however, they were seeking to escape from the rising water which was gradually filling their runs.

The two young boys, with barely enough energy left to speak and the water beginning to creep up the lengths of their trouser legs, could hear the rodents dashing about in the darkness in a desperate attempt to find a safe place.

"I'm frightened Fred, where is dad?   Will the rats bite us Fred?" pleaded the little lad, seeking some comfort from his brother and father.

"I'm-by'ere-Hugh-bach," he heard his father's strained voice between desperate deep breaths, his energy all but spent.   "u-'old-on-to-Fred—there-is-a-good-boy,-an'-u'll-be-olright.   The-rats-'on't-bite-'u-bach-they'll-just-run-about,-----'u-just-cwtch-in-with-Fred-now-an'-try-to-go-to-sleep dad's-by-ere-so-don't-'u-worry-now."

Andrew Lloyd was fighting to breathe with his last effort of resistance; yet cursing his inability to even reach out and offer an arm of comfort to his boys.

Young Fred was also hardly able to stay conscious; closing his eyes he was very soon lost in an abyss of total fatigue. But little Hugh, while also fighting against a natural inclination to lose consciousness, could still hear the rats and occasionally feel them as one or two run over his body. Gripped as he was by the hand of terror, as a rat run across his face, he let out a final muffled scream before his mind and body gave way to the inevitable.

But no one heard Hugh Lloyd's scream; he was the last to remain conscious, and within a half hour or so of his losing consciousness the water completely engulfed all twenty-five victims.

Harding had earlier written his final words in his notebook, aware that he would soon be overpowered by nature. He placed the notebook sealed in the way he had intended in the inside pocket of his coat; his final conscious act. His last words, though never a religious man were: "God help us."

11

At the moment of the explosion it was Dewi Baker who had set the hooter in motion, which had instantly brought back the memory of the terrible day he lost his son. His thoughts, however, quickly turned to the young boys now trapped in the mine, who may perhaps meet with the same fate.

The few other surface workers came running towards the mine portal - having witnessed the huge ball of fire, like that from the mythical dragon's mouth; propel itself out of the mine into the air- aghast at the sight of the mine's complete blockage. Within an hour or so a team of rescuers consisting of volunteer miners from other mines in the valley, were on the scene along with the General Manager and the Overman. Many of the villagers had also arrived in response to the all-too-familiar sound of the warning hooter.

Under instructions the surface workers had set up a barrier to keep the people away from the working area. It wasn't long before Peter Driscoll arrived having to thread his way through the anguished crowd; he assured them that everything possible would be done to release the workers but that, having not yet inspected the site, he was not in a position to make a commitment regarding the time this might take. He appealed to them to remain behind the barrier so that the rescuers could work unimpeded. With that he proceeded to the mine portal.

Steve Parfitt stood alongside the General Manager as Peter Driscoll arrived. He had been to see Leslie Eaton earlier, on his errand to convey the workers' complaint and threat to withdraw their labour over the air–flow problem. The two men had just reiterated the matter and agreed that now was not the time to raise the subject, which might prove highly contentious. Parfitt was, quietly confident however, that it was unlikely that the general public were aware of the failure to cut the Return Airway or Air Shaft or even what a Return Airway was; such things he assumed; would be discussed only among the miners themselves and until recently had not been an issue.

For the moment he had a heavier cross to bear -though tempered by an undoubted sense of relief- in the knowledge that had the earlier dispute not arisen and he been obliged to respond to the workers' demands, he too would now be either trapped or dead within the mine; he could barely contain his emotions. To add to this, he was convinced that the air-flow issue must surely be raised in an official investigation at a later date, when he might well be called to give evidence. For the moment, however, he could do nothing but wait and hope that the men will be saved.

However, as the hours passed by it soon became apparent that despite their unrelenting efforts, the volunteer rescuers were making comparatively little progress. Among them were a couple of men experienced in this type of operation. It was their appointed leader, Gerwyn James, who approached Peter Driscoll and Leslie Eaton, who were standing close by. Introducing himself, he politely addressed the two men.

"Excuse me gentlemen, my name is Gerwyn James and I am the appointed Leader of the rescue team. Could I have a word concerning the present state of progress?"

"Of course, of course Mr James,' responded the Engineer. "What can you tell us of your progress and the likelihood of getting into the mine soon?"

"I regret sir that progress has been very slow and consequently, it is possible that we will not be able to gain access to the mine at all. Based upon my experience in dealing'with similar minin' falls, I believe this mine has been completely lost. It appears that the rock which we are attemptin' to penetrate is not of loose boulders, as is common in such cases, but of one solid mass extendin' a considerable distance into the mine and possibly the entire mine."

"Good heavens, Mr James," the Engineer responded alarmingly, "are you suggesting that we abandon the rescue operation already?"

"No, no Mr Driscoll, sir," Gerwyn James replied, "It's not my place to make suggestions. I am merely pointing out the dilemma we are faced with. Any suggestions or decisions must come from 'u gentlemen; I can assure 'u that there is not one man here who would wish to quit if there was the remotest chance of success."

This was the least encouraging news the two officials wanted to hear and Steve Parfitt was enduring his own private anxieties. They knew full well that any indication of abandoning the rescue operation at this early stage would be met with alarming response from the villagers and could even insight an uncontrollable reaction.

"We must ask you to carry on with the task, Mr James, and consider the position as you progress," said the Engineer, "it might prove that the fall is less extensive than you imagine and you will make a break through soon."

"Very well sir, I'm sorry to appear so pessimistic but I can only relate what is mine and the other experienced rescuers opinions; let us hope that we are wrong."

Thus, Gerwyn James returned to the working area and informed the men that the officials had given the order to keep working in the hope of a breakthrough. As no one wished to give up, they resumed with as much commitment as they had shown from the start.

Due to the lack of useful lighting, when darkness fell which, it being January, was early evening, progress was greatly impaired. Nonetheless, the work did continue throughout the hours of darkness with the aid of whatever artificial lighting the team could muster.

By the morning of the fourth day with still comparatively limited progress, a meeting between the leading rescuers, the Engineer and General Manager, resolved to address the villagers and explain the situation as best they could; there was no option but to present the facts and not try to cover up the truth.

None of the villagers had left the scene since the hooter had brought them rushing up the mountainside; cooking on makeshift paraffin stoves and sleeping on and under rough blankets. By now the bitterly cold weather must also have been taking its toll but no one complained or had any intention of leaving; no physical discomfort could compare with the absolute distress they were enduring, not knowing if their men would be saved or lost.

As they witnessed the party of officials and rescuers walking towards the barrier, which had contained them up to now, a sudden surge of bodies sent the barrier crashing to the ground. Peter Driscoll dashed ahead of the others and holding both hands high in the air appealed to the crowd to stay where they were. They stopped when he came face to face with them and raised his hand as a gesture of calm.

When the others had caught up with him the Engineer called for attention and began to address the forlorn faces, a task he must surely have dreaded. Nonetheless, he determined to say it as it was and not attempt to raise false hope.

"Ladies and gentlemen, it is my sad duty to point out to you that having reached the fourth day of continuous battle against the fall, the rescue team are forced to concede that they are not winning. It is the conclusion of the men and their leaders, after much deliberation, that there is every chance that the mine has completely collapsed and the likelihood of reaching the miners is extremely doubtful. It would appear that the rock confronting the rescuers is of a solid mass and not, as I am reliably informed, of loose boulders, common in such cases."

Almost without notice Squire William Watkins, and two representatives of the colliery Owner/Shareholders arrived at the scene. Having learned of the explosion they had purposely stayed away up to now, conscious that only those with mining experience could handle such a situation and that they might in fact get in the way; this was their first visit to the mine, the practical operating of which was outside their role or knowledge. Their arrival interrupted the Engineer's announcement but the Squire beckoned him continue.

The two Owner/Shareholders stood alongside the Squire, General Manager and the Overman, perhaps trying to be as discrete as possible, aware that they would be completely unknown, not only by the villagers but the workers as well. The business office that governed the finances: costs and profits of not just Pentrebach mine but several others in the area covering the three Squires' lands, was based at Cardiff and the two Owner/Shareholders were part of the complement of that office.

The Engineer raising his arms apologised for the interruption and continued.

"As I was explaining, the rescuers have been working for several days nonstop and have concluded that the barrier they face does seem insurmountable. The General Manager and I have discussed the matter with the most experienced men in the team who have arrived at a decision which is, that there is but one option left open to them, but it is in itself fraught with danger. That option is to use dynamite in an attempt to break what seems to be an impenetrable obstacle. However, before they commit to this action they wish to emphasize that such a process could well create a further and more powerful gas explosion, whereby the mine would unquestionably be lost. And even if the dynamite does not trigger off any gas, it might well reveal that the mine was already completely and irretrievably sealed. That is why it was decided to inform you of the desperate position we find ourselves in.

"After much debate the team and we officials have decided that to resort to explosives is the only option left and that we must therefore, ask you to be aware of this and move further back, where the barrier will be replaced for extra safety and you will be prepared for the effects of the explosions to follow."

The effect of this terrible news, which clearly illustrated that the rescue attempt appeared to be failing; now down to a final desperate last option, had devastated the weary and distraught villagers.

Alice Jones, husband of Wally Jones and mother of the two young lads; Ken and Brian stepped forward and walked up close to the Squire looking him straight in the face.

"My 'usband and my two boys are in there Mr Watkins; can't 'u offer them any 'ope other than to blow the place up?"

The Squire had up to now hardly ever come into contact with the colliers, let alone their wives. This must have been the most difficult moment of his life. However, before he could answer, Alice Jones had to be helped away, a crumbling tragic wreck.

The Squire was visibly moved by this direct face to face approach and lowered his head seeking refuge behind the officials.

However, the three Irish wives, Kathleen O'Grady, Caroline Donovan and Mavis O'Connor pushed their way forward also to confront the Squire, and surprising not only him but the other officials and the

Owner/Shareholders —even though she did not know who the were- Carolyn Donovan asked him why there was only one way in and out of the mine.

For a moment no one offered an answer, when the General Manager stepped forward and called the three women one side.

"Ladies please, it is not the Squire's place to respond to that question, he has never had any control over the running of the mine; he merely owns the land. I would, therefore, suggest that today is not the day to look for answers but I can promise you a full explanation will be forthcoming later. Please let us get on with the rescue mission and leave such matters for a more appropriate time?"

With this the three women walked away but Leslie Eaton was now well aware that the airflow issue would without doubt come back to haunt him. Steve Parfitt, who was within hearing distance, although not noticed, had gone quite pale and was shivering within; so he had been wrong in believing the villagers knew nothing of the airflow question. He was, like the General Manager, sure of the day of reckoning.

The decision to use dynamite as a last resort, had affected many of the women: mothers, sisters and girlfriends alike. Mabel Llewellyn, whose father and boyfriend were in the mine, had all but collapsed, her mother, desperately trying to support her. The scene was one of anguish and misery, here and there family groups huddled together completely traumatised and filled with the hopelessness of their inability to make any difference.

With the barrier moved to a safe distance and the villagers all gathered behind it the tension was almost visible.

And so the blasting began. The first explosion, which was very loud, must have shaken those behind the barrier through to their souls. Smoke and dust flew in all directions, for a while blotting out any sight of the mine from the onlookers. As the air began to clear, the rescue team and the officials with the Squire and the two Owner/Shareholders in close pursuit, moved towards the mine to inspect the effect of the dynamite. It was Gerwyn James who reached the mine portal first; his face however, needed no voice to confirm his response.

With little more than a couple yards progress made, the rescue team were well aware that to continue blasting held little hope and that the time had perhaps come to accept that Pentrebach Level was lost forever. But who was going to make the decision to call a halt and abandon all further attempts to liberate the miners?

The now desperate officials, ever aware that they were clutching at straws, went on to order a further two attempts in the belief that they had to demonstrate the futility of their efforts. Alas, as the dust from the third blast was clearing revealing a further disappointment, Gerwyn James could be seen talking to Peter Driscoll and Leslie Eaton.

"Gentlemen, I must ask 'u to come to a decision. We are now in the fourth day of this rescue operation and still up against a blank wall. It would be more than optimistic to believe that anyone has survived in that mine. Even if the mine has not completely caved in, by now the water will have filled whatever space there might be behind the fall; to continue would only foster false hope and add to the already miserable sufferin' the families and villagers are having to cope with."

"I am afraid Mr James is right," said the Engineer, "we have surely reached the end of our efforts. We must confront these poor people with the reality that the miners of Pentrebach Level are truly lost."

"This most painful duty must fall to me." The Squire declared. "But how does one announce such a finality to bear upon a whole community?"

With these words of deep melancholy the Squire walked off in the direction of the crowd waiting in sombre silence behind the barrier. The others followed on slowly and meekly. As the Squire reached the barrier his sad declaration was pre-empted by the waiting villagers; his expression and that of those in close pursuit with bowed heads, foretelling the news.

The sudden and vehement wailing of the women was soon to confirm the conclusion of the Squire's devastating message. However, the villagers made no effort to leave and, in fact, proceeded en masse in the direction of the mine pushing past the officials, the Squire and the Owner/Shareholders. When they reached the mine and could see for themselves what limited progress the rescue workers efforts, after four days and despite the three attempts at blasting their way in, had achieved and the blank wall of rock that faced them, they stopped and gathered together with heads bowed in an act of acceptance and deference.

It was the vicar who led them in prayer which was succeeded by an overwhelming expression of collective grief; the women and children hugging each other and sharing their sorrow; a more pitiful and desperate sight would be hard to imagine.

It took some time to persuade the villagers to leave the site; some of the women stood staring at the mine entrance, as if by some miracle the miners would suddenly remove the barrier and walk out. The Squire, Owner/Shareholders and the officials pleaded with the men to speak to the women in an attempt to prevail upon them that there was nothing to be gained by staying there.

Meanwhile, Gwladys Bishop approached the two unknown gentlemen.

"Excuse me gentlemen could I be so bold as to ask who 'u are? I'm guessing that 'u 'ave somethin' to do with the mine or 'u wouldn't be 'ere?"

One of them, a tall man with an unfamiliar accent; Welsh, but not of the valleys, began by offering his and his colleague's condolences for the great loss that this tragic day had witnessed.

"We represent the Owners and Shareholders of the company that cover the Pentrebach Level and many other mines in the area, madam, and I can assure you that we share in your terrible grief here today. There will be an official Inquiry at a later date when I sincerely hope we can uncover the cause of this unprecedented accident and thereby prevent anything like it happening again. I regret, however, that we cannot offer you any explanation or comfort at this time, as we are as much in the dark as you are."

"Beggin' u're pardon sir, but I think 'u are much more in the dark than we are. We 'ave lived with the lives of miners over many years; we 'ave witnessed accidents down through those years and many of us 'ave nursed severely injured men from time to time and some among us 'ave lost men underground before; but none of us 'ave ever experienced anythin' like this. 'u can 'ave as many Inquiries as 'u like sir, but it won't bring any of those men or boys back now will it? Somethin' 'appened 'ere at Pentrebach that will carry great pain and grief with us for the rest of our lives; 'u sir can never begin to share that kind of burden. Pentrebach will soon become nothin' more than an entry in 'u're company's books and when the books are closed so will the events of this tragedy be. It will be the loss of money to the company that will be 'u're greatest pain."

It was plain that the gentleman was grossly embarrassed and quite unable to respond. Luckily, Gwladys Bishop walked away to join the other villagers, granting this unknown figure of business the relief of his unprepared for predicament; one which he would without doubt remember for a very long time.

Gradually, the people all gathered together and began the slow trudge down the mountainside to their homes; many of them would now be without a husband, brother or son or, as in the case of the Bishops, Joneses and Lloyds, husbands and sons. Life for many was never going to be the same, especially as there will be no bodies; no coffins; no burials. Theirs was an empty grieving; a chasm of despair.

12

In a rare instance the relatives and villagers were allowed to attend the Official Inquiry into the disaster, though they were instructed that they may not interrupt the proceedings. It was perfectly understandable that the question of why the Return Airway or Shaft had not been cut which might have saved the miners –had they been trapped and not lost beneath the fall- was raised.

The Overman, Steve Parfitt, as he had predicted, was called as a witness. He told the Inquiry that on the morning of the explosion the men had expressed their concern over the air-flow in strong terms, even threatening to withdraw their labour unless something was done. He had at their request taken the matter up with Mr Leslie Eaton the colliery General Manager, within an hour. Mr Eaton had assured him that the matter would be passed on to Mr Driscoll the Mining Engineer, and confirmed that the hard heading team, which had been fully engaged in a project in the other valley, would shortly be available to start work on the Return Airway at Pentrebach.

"But even as we spoke," Parfitt continued, "we were interrupted by the piercing sound of the Pentrebach

Level 'ooter alerting us that somethin' serious had 'appened at the mine."

The next witness was Mr Leslie Eaton, who confirmed everything that Parfitt had said and went on to explain why there had been a delay in the making of a Return Airway or Shaft at Pentrebach Level.

"It is customary in all new mines," he began, "to delay the cutting of a Return Airway for some time in order to establish the value of the mine before engaging in such a non-profit making work. Should a mine prove to be unsatisfactory the expense of cutting a Return Airway would only add to the losses incurred.

At that moment a female voice from the gallery clearly interrupted Leslie Eaton.

"So it was money that took our boys lives then, Mr Eaton, was it?

At first there was an uneasy silence, this bold remark taking the general manager completely by surprise.

However, the presiding judge broke the silence with a sharp response.

"Whoever it was who spoke out then will be removed from the court if there is a recurrence. We have already made an exception in allowing members of the public to attend these proceedings, which are usually held in a closed court. I can assure you that all aspects of the events relating to this terrible tragedy will be dealt with and if there has been any breech of the law that affected the outcome, the offenders will be subject to appropriate action. I must, therefore, insist that only those called upon to give evidence will be heard; please, no more outbursts."

With that the proceedings were allowed to go on uninterrupted but it was likely that Leslie Eaton and others, involved in the running of Pentrebach Level, were affected, even by this solitary remark. There is no doubt that Squire Watkins, despite his not having any role to play in the running of the mine, as a recipient of its benefits, must also have had a twinge of conscience.

Leslie Eaton was asked to continue:

"Mr Parfitt the Overman and previous witness did report an unusual smell at the mine in late August. He and I carried out a standard air and gas check but found nothing unusual and the lamp reading gave no indication of any problem. The smell we concluded was as a result of small pockets of air lying above the lagging in the Main. Mr Driscoll, the engineer and I carried out further checks later and came to the same conclusion.

"In September we had a very unfortunate accident when a young lad, Clive Baker, was killed under a totally unpredictable fall. This of course affected the men and indeed all those connected with the mine.

"Some weeks later the mine met with a geological Fault, which took a few weeks to deal with and resulted in the coalface veering to the right, making a sudden change in direction and thus necessitating the re-establishing of the stalls, before normal working conditions could be resumed. It was sometime after the Fault that the men began to refer to the airflow as being a problem.

"Mr Driscoll and I discussed the matter of an air Return or Shaft with a team of specialist workers who were currently engaged in a job at a mine in the neighbouring valley who agreed to begin work at Pentrebach Level as soon as they were available This was just before the Christmas break and so no further communication with this team could be made until after Christmas, when they informed us that they would be able to begin work in early February.

"Regrettably, it was on the day of the explosion that Mr Parfitt arrived at my house to inform me of the miners' serious complaint over the airflow and, as he has already explained, it was, therefore, circumstances that overtook any appropriate action I and my colleagues might have initiated as a result."

Mr Driscoll, the colliery engineer, was next called to give evidence, confirmed that there was every intention of making a start on the Return Airway as soon as the hard heading team had finished in the other valley; which was predicted to be as early February.

The geologist who had attended the mine at the time of the Fault also gave evidence. He pointed out that it was an unusual Fault which had affected the both the width and alignment of the coalface and had caused a considerable delay in production. When work did re-commence the face was drifting to the right.

The response from the presiding judge was to confirm that it was not uncommon in 'new' mines to delay the cutting of a Return Airway or Air Shaft nor was it unlawful. He also emphasized that the colliery management was keen to get this work done but had been prevented from so doing due to the appropriately skilled work force not being readily available. And it was also accepted that the unexpected Fault would have been a cause for concern and a need of immediate attention and delay.

Nevertheless, the judge –who did appear to indicate that perhaps an opportunity had been missed- pointed out that there were mine owners in the area that had made air shafts early in their mines' history and that this practice may one day become obligatory. However, he went on to say that it was not the court's place to make judgement by pre-emption and as a consequence, no blame or responsibility for these 'unfortunate' and 'regrettable' circumstances could be attributed to the colliery management or land owners.

The Squire was given an opportunity to speak but he made no reference to the cause of the accident pointing out that as a landowner he was but a business associate. He went on to offer his sincere condolences to the relatives of the deceased and to confirm that it had been agreed between himself and all those financially involved, that the entire colliery and all its appurtenance will remain in situ and a barrier fence with a memorial plaque attached will be raised around the area, in respect of and deference to the lost miners.

There were many villagers who were not happy with the outcome of this Inquiry and felt that the failure to cut an Airway should not have been dismissed so readily; but they did believe that the judge had been sympathetic to their view. They questioned the moral issue; why didn't the Squire and his business associates give the matter of the miners' safety and wellbeing priority over profit? However, having no means to challenge the authority of the ruling body or any means of recourse, their dissatisfaction could only be expressed in the home or the pub.

Some months after the Inquiry, a memorial service was held at Pentrebach Level colliery site, in recognition of those lost in the colliery disaster. The entire village population attended, even the children. Also in attendance were Squire William Watkins and his son Rees and, of course, Peter Driscoll and Leslie Eaton accompanied by Steve Parfitt. The Owner/Shareholders were conspicuous in their absence. It was these five who stood just behind the vicar of Pentrebach church, who conducted the service. The service was a very sombre affair during which, a number of volunteer members of the families of the lost miners stood in turns, to express their feelings and speak of the loved ones they had lost.

It was Gwladys Bishop –last of the villagers to speak- who, after expressing the devastating grief and burden of losing her wonderful husband and son, had the courage to conclude with a careful hint with regard to the absence of the Return Airway.

"–Of course, I don't understand the way a colliery works as well as any of the men 'ere do. But I will always wonder if our men and boys might still be 'ere if, as it 'as been suggested, somethings had been attended to earlier."

This brought the service to a close but must have created a degree of discomfort for the mining officials and, indeed the Watkins family.

Of course it was not grief alone that the wives of the lost miners had to bear. With the loss of the breadwinner and in some cases a working son too, they were about to face a life of severe impoverishment or even destitution, when they would be forced to find some form of employment, usually in the capacity of domestic service to the better off; as the Watkins' household for example.

It took many years for the Pentrebach Level disaster to not be continually referred to in the village homes and Inn and why, in late 1955 (ninety-two years on) when the National Coal Board decided they wanted to open a new mine in the vicinity of the old Level, there was, initially, considerable opposition to it.

13

Preliminary boring took place at the location of what was to be the Pentrebach New Drift in November 1955 in preparation for excavating the main heading. While bituminous coal was still widely used domestically and for steam power in a number of industries, the NCB was confident of a buoyant market.

Establishing the drift and all the necessary buildings and equipment, the inclined dram-road with its weight and gravity system; plus a lamp-room, pithead baths and ambulance station on site, and the screening plant near the valley railway line for immediate distribution, was to take just under a year with the colliery opening for production in October 1956.

The general appearance of the original village of Pentrebach had not changed dramatically since the time of the Pentrebach Level but the mining methods and general conditions in the mines had. By now no boy under the age of sixteen was allowed to work in a coalmine and before he could, he would have undergone a four month training schedule at one of the NCB's specially adapted Training Centres.

Here the boys were to experience conditions in either specially adapted buildings or in a disused colliery in the form of a mock coal mine. There would be workshops and canteen facilities on the site as well. The programme would involve alternate weeks at the mock mine and at a classroom set aside at a local Technical College or other academic establishment. The lessons were nonetheless very basic, with no exams or follow on training.

The long established traditional pillar and stall mining practice had been replaced by the continuous chain or belt conveyor coalface known as longwall mining. Besides this, no collier had to hole out under the coal anymore; a mechanical cutter did the job for him. A coalface, of which there may be more than one and depending upon its length, could contain any number of men working alongside each other; each man would have his 'stent' of coal, which was customarily eight yards long, ten yards if he had a boy with him.

Two 'roads' led to the coalface. The road at the head of the conveyor where the coal tipped onto another conveyor carrying it to the 'Dump,' was called the Gate Road; the other end where the conveyor motor stood, was the Supply Road, where material for supporting the top was brought to meet the colliers' and coggers' needs. The sides of the roads were lined with 'packs' or 'packwalls' which were built out of waste stones and infilled with all manner of waste material. A pack must be tight from the base or 'thill' to the top and must extend at least six feet from the road into the 'gob' which is the area left open after the coal has been extracted. This gob space could sometimes extend many yards before finally giving way to the weight of the exposed area.

Gone were the days when a miner would work a sixteen hour day, miners now worked shifts of eight hours. In most collieries there was a three shift system. The coal was cut on the Night shift while at the same time the 'coggers' would replace the cog supports behind the conveyor. A cog or chock consisted of timbers approximately four feet long and four inches in diameter -or square- tapered at either end to create stability. They would be laid one upon another in the shape of a square until just short of the top, where wooden wedges would be forced in to secure the structure. The colliers working on the Day shift cleared the coal and secured the coalface with timber posts and wedges or timber posts and metal flats; to cover more space. It was the job of the Afternoon shift workers to move the conveyor on to catch up with the coalface each day. This procedure was known as the 'Turnover.'

The New Pentrebach Drift operated the conveyor face system with at the time two conveyors –the one in the coal face being a chain conveyor – the other of rubber-belt carrying the coal to the Dump. Here the coal fell into the drams which were moved on as they filled until a 'journey,' consisting of up to eighteen drams, was complete. The main haulage was powered by electricity but horses were still used during maintenance work and in roads –the supply road for instance – not connected with the extraction of coal. Electricity had improved the mining industry, the conveyor motors were powered by electricity and the cutter that undercut the coal and so were the power drills and of course the miners' cap-lamps by battery-stored electricity.

While the old Pentrebach village layout had not altered very much; all the original streets being as they were at the time of the first mine. The houses had, nonetheless, been updated to include running water, bathrooms and indoor toilets, etc. The back-to backs of Riverside Row had been completely updated in that the central dividing wall running the whole length of the street had been removed piecemeal and where originally there were two houses joined in the middle there now was one; thus no more back-to-backs. Other buildings had, however, been constructed to make for a much bigger village: the Miners' Welfare Hall, a cinema a library and, of course, many more shops and one other public house called the Miners' Arms. But the most significant addition was a large council house estate erected under the Atlee housing programme just after the Second World War.

Afon Manor House, which once belonged to the Watkins family, had been abandoned since 1912 when Rees Watkins, the last squire died; his wife having predeceased him and his two daughters –there being no male heir – married into wealthy families and moved away. As a consequence the people of Pentrebach knew nothing of their current lives.

The canal was still visible but in parts choked with reeds, having long since given way to the railway. In addition there was now a very good road running through the valley.

Pentrebach New Drift employed men from in and around the village and within six months it was as productive as some of the smaller established mines in the area. However, some of the colliers had begun to notice a change in the colour of the coalface. This unusual anomaly was brought to the attention of senior management resulting in Mr Jeffery Maddocks, the company's geologist, being brought in to investigate. No one less suited to the environment could be imagined than Jeffrey Maddocks who was rarely out of his white shirt and tie. It was obvious that he found the surroundings totally out of his comfort zone.

Accompanying Mr Maddocks at the coalface were Collin Wright, Colliery Manager and Walter Francis, Colliery Undermanager.

The two colliers, who had reported the peculiarity, Desmond Richards and Oliver Hardwick, were alongside them pointing out the distinct mixture of blue and gold, that was running through the seam.

"What do you make of it Jeffery?" the manager asked the geologist.

"I have never actually seen it in a mine Collin. However, it suggests to me that there is a considerable presence of water in the coal as this is the effect water permeating coal has; but where can it be coming from?"

"If I may interrupt for a moment gentlemen," said Oliver Hardwick, "that's exactly what Llew Gardner, the oldest collier workin' 'ere said. Apparently he 'ad seen it in another mine many years ago. And he told us that it was followed by an inrush of water and that the men were lucky to get out alive."

"Well that's very interesting, Oliver, if not a little alarming," the manager remarked. "Do you think that's feasible Jeffery?"

"There have been a number of incidents of water inrush historically, usually as a result of old workings, generally Victorian, not being recorded and when abandoned, filling with water. Thus a later mine would unsuspectingly burst upon the unrecorded mine. Is it possible, Collin, that such a mine might exists ahead of you?"

"The only mine ever known to have operated in this vicinity, Jeffery, is the Old Pentrebach Level but, as you know, we have calculated that this mine is progressing at least a hundred yards to the north of the old level and should not come anywhere near whatever might remain of it, if it did in fact survive at all."

"I can only think of one thing we can do Collin," the undermanager proposed. "Get the longest drill we have and bore into the seam and continue to do so before each cutting. If any amount of water comes through the bore hole we will be forewarned and will have to consider the position then."

The manager agreed that this seemed a sensible approach. Consequently, the night shift men operating the cutter were instructed to bore with the longest drill available and to report to the night shift Overman should any water be detected seeping through the bore hole. If water was detected they were, of course, not to proceed with the cutting.

The drill used was five feet in length, driven in to its extremity each time. And on the third night of boring as they began to extract the drill, water was detected dribbling out of the bore hole. The cutter men, leaving the drill within the bore-hole sent for the Overman as instructed. Thus all work was suspended until the day shift when the three officials, Collin Wright, Walter Francis and Jeffrey Maddocks returned to the mine.

As the bore hole, even with the drill inside, had allowed some water to escape during the interim period, the immediate job was to find a suitable plug to stem the flow after the drill had been fully removed.

Within a short time a suitably tapered wooden plug had been cut to size and as the drill was carefully withdrawn by Oliver Hardwick, Desmond Richards stood by ready to insert the plug. Working in harmony the two colliers managed to successfully block the bore hole; but for how long?

"I'm not altogether convinced that that plug is going to hold back the water for very long Walter." The manager suggested, speaking to the undermanager. "Goodness knows just how much water is back there."

In apprehension of the danger of a possible imminent inrush, the manager ordered that everyone leave the mine until an official inspection was carried out and the water brought under control. Thus the mine was closed down until further notice. After a discussion between the NUM representatives and management, it was agreed that for the time being while the colliers were idle, they would receive the basic 'Day Wage' which was that paid to auxiliary and surface workers; who were the lowest paid operatives.

Back at the coalface, after removing the wooden plug, a steel pipe attached to a rubber hose was very quickly inserted into the bore hole from where the water was now running freely. This hose was itself connected to a wider pipe which fed the water with the aid of a pump to the surface of the mine where it was allowed to run down the mountainside. A small group of colliers were engaged in boring a series of further similar holes at the base of the coalface for the length of the face, all of which being attached to hoses and pipes. Therefore, eventually, a row of pipes emerged from the mine discharging hundreds of gallons of water every day.

For over a week the water flowed constantly from all the pipes; when suddenly, first one and then each one in turn saw the water peter out. Desmond Richards and Oliver Hardwick were called back into the mine and instructed to remove a section of the coal to determine where the water had been coming from. The process was conducted under very careful supervision with every safety precaution being taken.

It didn't take long for the two men to cut a gap, two yards wide and the length of the drill forward, when they could see that beyond this there was a gaping open space. Apart from the colliers, once again Collin Wright, Walter Francis and the reluctant Jeffrey Maddocks were present. It was they who, with the use of their spot cap lamps, proceeded through the cutaway into the open space.

The first thing they encountered was a dram road. The method in which the dram road had been laid down indicted that it had been there for many years. Apart from that it was buckled and twisted; the result of geological pressure over a long period of time.

Soon the five men were standing in the middle of the dram road, looking all about. It was quickly determined that the seam of coal had somehow drifted to the right where there was clear evidence of early workings. It would appear that a geological upheaval had occurred effecting the course of the coal seam.

"Well, well," Jeffrey Madocks declared, perhaps now feeling that there had been a purpose in his presence after all. "It would appear Collin that your mine is going to have to turn if you wish to follow the coal. There has been a geological disturbance known as a Balk Fault running some distance behind us, caused by denudation, where a channel or wash has been filled in when the bed now forming the roof (top) of the coal seam was deposited. That lying above the top is sandstone which filled the depression squeezing the coal seam almost to the bottom or thill. Balk faults can vary in length and width considerably and are not that common. Here it would appear that the coal was almost completely lost for some distance and when the seam was regained the miners found they had experienced a change in direction. This may explain why you came upon it by surprise."

It's doubtful that everyone clearly understood Madocks' explanation but he had been given the opportunity to demonstrate his geological knowledge.

The dram road ran only a short distance to the right where it could be clearly seen that the coal had been worked, as a number of pillar and stall settings were visible but appeared as if they had been vacated suddenly; there being half filled drams and no sign of any tools. It was when the men turned from the coal face to study the dram road running away from them that they discovered it went on for quite some distance; well beyond the beam of even the officials' cap lamps.

"What mine can this be?" Jeffrey Maddocks enquired.

"I have a strong suspicion that we have, despite my earlier dismissal of it, actually entered the old Pentrebach Level," said the manager. "It would appear that due to the Fault, they were as you say Jeffrey, forced to change direction bringing them accidentally in line with our path."

This revelation sent a shiver down the spines of the five men, for if this was the Pentrebach Level then they were all aware that there was every chance if they proceeded along the dram road, they would come to the location of the remains of the lost miners of 1863.

"If this is the old Pentrebach Level," the manager exclaimed, "then when the explosion occurred the men must have left the coalface to investigate. How far it is from here to where the mine was sealed I can't say and whether we will be able to progress along the dram road without encountering any roof falls or other disturbances and/or obstacles, we can't know. However, it must have been near where the mine was sealed that they will have gathered and attempted to dig their way out. Of course what we do know is that from the portal in, the rock that sealed the mine was impenetrable, which is why the miners failed to get out and the would-be rescuers failed to get in."

Fortunately, the current water seepage was minimal, so they were able to proceed safely.

"We will proceed cautiously," said the manager, "and if our way is not barred, try to reach the spot where the cave-in took place. If, as is likely, we come across any human remains, nothing must be touched; we will leave things as they are until we contact the National Coal Board Executives for a decision."

They moved along stealthily the three officials keeping slightly ahead of the two colliers. But, as was suspected by the manager, they did encounter certain obstacles. At times they had to stoop to pass under places where the top had been lowered due to years of pressure and in other locations the dram road raised from the same cause. Nevertheless, they went on and after some fifty minutes or so they arrived at a double parting beyond which the manager's spotlight caught a glimpse of something white; which made the party instinctively come to a halt. It soon became clear that they were looking at the skeletons of four ponies. On closer examination they could detect that the ponies had been tethered as the leather ties were still attached to four separate posts.

"They must have been left here out of the way while the men went to investigate the explosion." The manager suggested.

A short distance further and the three brightest lights scanning ahead revealed several human remains; some still exhibiting bits of clothing, boots and belts; amazing after so long submerged under water. However, for the most part they were no more than skeletons.

"This is as far as we go gentlemen," the manager declared. "It looks quite certain we are in the old Pentrebach Level, let us return to the surface and consult with a higher authority when a detailed survey can be carried out to establish if we are right and what action should then be taken."

14

As they left the scene the manager paused for a moment and spoke to the others, expressing the need to keep the discovery of the Pentrebach Level a secret until he has had the opportunity to consult the NCB.

"I look to your confidence in this matter because to reveal publicly the discovery of the lost miners' remains before we are absolutely certain that that is what we have discovered, might create repercussions throughout the village; aware as we all are that the matter of the disaster is still a very sensitive subject."

They were, of course only too happy to agree not to mention the revelation until it was officially approved.

Before the manager set off to engage in contacting the appropriate people, he had asked that Richards and Hardwick with one appointed fitter, set up a pump near the coalface of the old mine, with a pipe connected to the new mine in order to keep the water level down; thankfully the water seepage was only gradual but they would need the place to be clear of water to accommodate access for the eventual official inspection.

The setting up of the pump was arranged by the next day and shortly afterwards, just two officials: Collin Wright and Walter Francis returned; Jeffrey Maddocks, perhaps gratefully, was not asked to join them.

The business of arranging an official inspection of the old mine, including representatives from the Home Office, was to take some time. This time was not however wasted, as the manager arranged for a group of specialist workers to attend to make the old mine roadway safe. This involved removing the rails and levelling the ground beneath, clearing any fallen debris and replacing supports, etc.

Before these specialist workers arrived the manager called upon Hardwick and Richards to erect a temporary brattice cover in order to conceal the area where the ponies' and miners' remains lay. The appointed workers were instructed to operate up to but not beyond this point.

Later Hardwick and Richards were called upon once more to inform them that they might be expected to join the inspection team in the event that some labour is required.

"There will shortly be an inspection of the old mine," the manager explained, "not only by representatives of the NCB but also some leading NUM officials, and some gentlemen from the Home Office, one of whom will be the chief medical officer, whose job it will be to determine what should be done about the human remains. You two will be allowed to attend but remain discretely out of the way and not under any circumstances address any member of the inspection party. If you are asked to assist in any way follow instructions very carefully."

Earlier, there had been considerable concern in the village over the protracted closure of the New Mine, which created much conjecture on the part of those who had not worked for such a long time as a result. The initial agreement by the NCB to pay those laid-off the basic "Day Wage" had not been sustained. The NCB, in consultation with the NUM, pointed out that while initially they envisaged a brief shut-down, it had now developed into a much more protracted one, consequently, to continue to pay idle men was not economically practical and that they were obliged to advise those affected, to register at the Employment Exchange until further notice.

This resulted in a bitter exchange between the two parties with, the NUM accusing the NCB of reneging on their promise and demanding to know what, exactly, was causing the failure to resume operations at the mine. Consequently, at a private meeting between the two colliery officials who had been involved in the discovery of what was now presumed to be the old Pentrebach Level and The NUM Lodge Chairman Max Forester with Lodge Secretary, Frank Lewis, the up-to-date position was revealed to the NUM leaders. The colliery manager went on to confirm that he had been in touch with the NCB and that this had led to them getting in touch with the Home Office and the delegating of appropriate people, who were soon to visit the mine and determine what to do about the human remains.

"Good heavens," Max Forester exclaimed. "If, as you believe, you have discovered the remains of those poor lost souls of the Pentrebach Level disaster, I'm afraid the decision of what to do will not be left entirely to those from London, Mr Wright; I've a strong suspicion that the people of Pentrebach will have something to say about it."

The manager, aware that Forester was given to expressing strong views and enforcing his members' opinions and those of the villagers' over all others, responded firmly but with a degree of tact.

"Please let us deal with this matter step by step, Max. I would emphasize that we are all obliged to adhere to the law; and it is only from Home Office guidance that we will learn exactly what laws govern this particular and undoubtedly very rare situation. Can I, therefore, rely on you not to make any suggestions or express your personal opinion in the presence of the Home Office gentlemen, but wait until they have carried out the inspection and formally announced their findings and decision?"

Forester, not wishing to ruffle any feathers during such a sensitive occasion, confirmed that he would not interfere with or in any way disrupt the proceedings on the day but would await the official outcome and consider the matter then. However, he expressed that he would be calling for a public meeting in the village should the Home Office make any attempt to remove and dispose of the remains without public knowledge.

While the manager was not happy with this pre-emptive approach by Forester he decided to let the matter rest for the time being.

15

As with all bureaucratic offices, the Home Office didn't seem to attach too much urgency in arranging a date for the inspection of the old mine, even though it was aware of the discovery of human remains and that the New Mine was temporarily shut down. Conveniently however, it did allow the necessary preparation at the old mine to be carried out. It was two weeks after the NCB had contacted the appropriate authority before three men by arrangement with the National Coal Board Executive, arrived at the mine. The complete complement of the party entering the New Mine en-route to the Old Mine that day consisted of:

Three Gentlemen from the Home Office including the Chief Medical Officer; Colliery Agent, Ken Gregory, Collin Wright and Walter Francis; Max Forester and Frank Lewis and just two colliers, Oliver Hardwick and Desmond Richards. Hardwick and Richards were brought along as 'labourers' in the event there would be some physical assistance needed.

After descending the New Mine the ten men proceeded through the opening that had been cut, revealing the dram road by now firmly believed to be that of the old Pentrebach Level. The rails had been moved to the sides of the road way by the appointed work force engaged by the manager. They paused here for the manager to explain to the visitors and others who had not been in this locality earlier, where it was presumed they were, pointing out the pillar and stall work which had been abandoned and also the reason why the coal face had suddenly changed direction.

"Now gentlemen," the manager continued, "if we proceed along this dram road, in the opposite direction we will arrive at the site of the human remains we came across during our initial visit; I wish to make it clear that I determined at that time not to disturb anything until an official party, as appointed here today, was approved and organised to carry out an authorised inspection and thereby determine the course of action that will be adopted."

The Home Office Medical Officer responded by agreeing that the manager had taken the right step at that time and expressed that upon the arrival at this site he would be obliged if he and his colleagues be allowed to carry out a preliminary inspection before consulting with those familiar with the area; that they might determine the true identity of the mine.

This was, of course, unanimously agreed.

Very little was said during the trudge up the dram road incline. However, as the first light fell upon the ponies' skeletons, the medical officer, very quietly remarked:

"I assume these are the animal remains you referred to Mr Wright, so we will move on as there is nothing to be gained from their examination."

"That's right Doctor, we are not far from the location of the lost miners now." The manager confirmed.

When they did reached the location of the first human skeletons, the Medical Officer asked the men to wait there while his team moved forward and began to inspect them, moving on from one to another up to a count of twenty-five. When they returned to the rest of the party the Medical Officer was carrying a small package and approached the manager.

"Mr Wright, this package was found in close proximity to one of the miners' remains; it has survived in apparent good condition and appears to have been purposely wrapped. Perhaps you should check it out later."

"Very well Doctor, we will investigate it later; it may be of no significance at all but one never knows."

"Well," the Medical Officer continued, "from what I have been told there were twenty-five miners, including four boys, lost in the Pentrebach Level disaster and as this tallies with the body count here, I believe we can be certain, gentlemen, that you have indeed uncovered the scene of that most tragic event of over ninety years past. I think it would be appropriate therefore, in the absence of a clergyman that we observe a minute's silence out of respect for these poor lost souls."

This was observed as the party all stood still with heads bowed.

When the minute was over, the manager suggested that they proceed to where the mine had been sealed by the explosion and examine the area for evidence of any attempt by the men to gain their release.

It wasn't far to the blocked mine but passing the twenty-five skeletons was a very unnerving experience; especially for the two miners who lived in the village. There was a pause when the party stopped at what was undoubtedly the skeleton of a boy; its dimensions much reduced when compared with those nearby; his boots and some pieces of tough material, as with the others, yet surviving in part, were somewhat smaller than most.

"Apparently," Max Forester declared, "the youngest victim was a boy of twelve, these could well be his remains; it hardly bears thinking about."

The party moved on in silence.

At the scene of the collapsed mine the tools: shovels, mandrels and sledgehammers, undoubtedly retrieved from the coalface to use in an attempt to break the soon to be discovered unbreakable rock, lay strewn about.

Evidence of what must have been a desperate effort on the part of the trapped men was clear. However, the futility of their efforts was also clear, as the face of the rock sealing the mine was that of one solid mass. The last three drams of a journey were visible before the sealed exit and the mining officials gathered round to examine them but their inspection was interrupted by the Medical Officer.

"Today, gentlemen," he declared, "I would suggest is not the day to carry out a physical inspection to determine what might have been the cause of the disaster; I'm sure that can be arranged at a later date. First, however, I think we should determine the procedure for the removal of the human remains, which will require careful handling."

"Of course," the manager agreed, "everything in its proper order."

"I would also suggest," the Medical Officer proposed, "that we return to the surface and discuss the matter formally, before I depart to make arrangements for the remains to be transported to an appropriate location for disposal."

The very word 'disposal' effected an immediate response from Max Forester, despite his earlier assurance that he would not make any suggestions or express a personal opinion, in the presence of the Home Office visitors.

"With respect sir," he declared, "what exactly do you mean by the 'disposal' of the remains? Am I to assume this operation is to be dealt with solely by some government department?"

The formality by way of introductions having been carried out before they entered the mine, the Medical Officer addressed the NUM Lodge Chairman by name.

"I'm not sure what your question implies, Mr Forester. The removal of the remains would need to be handled by qualified people and the government is surely best equipped to attend to that; and their later disposal would require legal authorisation, when again, the government could administer this operation without the need of any possible protracted legal delays."

At this point the manager interrupted, suggesting that these issues would be better discussed back in the office and called upon Max Forester to respect the position of the Medical Officer and his colleagues and not cause any unnecessary complications before an official meeting can be arranged.

"Very well, Mr Wright," responded Forester, "forgive my abruptness sir," he exclaimed, addressing the Medical Officer, "but I will be seeking a discussion on the matter at the earliest opportunity."

Nothing further was said, the manager encouraging the Medical Officer and his colleagues to hasten their return to the surface. As the party proceeded towards the colliery office, the two miners were thanked, discharged and sent home. But not before they had been instructed that under no circumstances were they to mention the discovery of the Pentrebach Level and of course the remains of the lost miners. If asked why the mine was to remain closed they could reveal the problem of the Fault and that they had been engaged in controlling the water level.

Upon their arrival at the office Collin Wright arranged the seating and opened the meeting by calling upon the Medical Officer –Doctor Carmichael- to express his findings and explain the course of action from here on. The Medical Officer began by thanking everyone for attending and explained that upon his return to London, after obtaining Home Office approval for the removal of human remains; just a couple of authorised people, myself included, with appropriate equipment would arrive at the mine when the skeletons of the deceased miners would be brought out and taken away for disposal, probably by burial or incineration. In view of the delicate nature of this operation it would be carried out in strict secrecy; with only a limited number of representatives from the National Coal Board, senior officers of the National Union of Mineworkers and those appointed to conduct the proceedings, being present. However, the physical removal of the human remains will require some labourers who would also be sworn to secrecy.

It was Max Forester who indicated that he would like to address the meeting first but Collin Wright got in immediately with the following.

"Before anyone responds to Doctor Carmichael's remarks I would like to relate to our visitors something of the tragic and somewhat unique circumstances surrounding the disaster that occurred at the Pentrebach Level in 1863 and the profound affect it had and continues to have upon the neighbouring village of that name."

By the time the manager had related, in somewhat protracted details, the story of the 1863 disaster, emphasising the affect this particular mining tragedy – where no one was saved and not a body recovered – had on the then community of Pentrebach and how even today, the disaster is treated as uniquely Pentrebach – the Home Office visitors began to appreciate the degree of sensitivity the subject provoked, as illustrated by Max Forester, when he questioned the 'disposal' of the human remains. This was exactly the intention of the manager's intervention.

In response, Doctor Carmichael, now in a much more condescending tone, proclaimed:

"Thank you Mr Wright, for that excellent and comprehensive account of what was undoubtedly a tragedy which appears to have left an indelible imprint upon the village of Pentrebach; I now understand why you, Mr Forester, are concerned with the procedure that will be adopted when the remains of the unfortunate miners are removed and disposed of. I can also appreciate that the term 'disposal of' could come across as somewhat clinical but I can assure you that it will, in fact, be carried out with the care and compassion it justly warrants."

"I am most grateful Doctor Carmichael," Forester responded, without waiting for official licence to speak, "for your acknowledgement of the need to treat the removal and custody of the lost miners' remains with the dignity and consideration they deserve. Can I therefore, put it to you, that far from the matter being kept secret, the whole of the community of Pentrebach be informed and a public meeting be arranged, that a decision on the proper placement of the remains be agreed upon? Before you respond Doctor," Forester hastened to add, "there is one particularly relevant issue, not strictly touched upon by Mr Wright that makes the Pentrebach disaster so different and why its consequences lay so heavily upon the village, even to this day.

"For three or four days the rescue team worked tirelessly and determinedly to break through to the trapped miners. Finally, they had no choice but to resort to dynamite even aware that this might bring about a further explosion. Alas, while there was no further explosion, the rock could not be penetrated and they were forced to abandon all attempts at rescue. It is the burden of *failure* that has weighed and continues to weigh so heavily upon the conscience of the Pentrebach village people. I believe that this chance discovery of the remains of the poor lost miners could offer an opportunity to ease that burden, if the village people are allowed to determine the final resting place of the recovered miners."

Doctor Carmichael paused for a while and everyone else, including Forester, sat in silent anticipation of the Medical Officer's response.

"First of all I must point out that there will be laws, Mr Forester, over which I will have no authority to counter, that might make yours and, should they agree, the villagers' desires and intentions prohibitive. The removal of any long term concealed human remains – with perhaps the exception of an archaeological dig- can only be sanctioned by the Home Office and is customarily carried out under strict and close scrutiny. It will, therefore, be my duty to seek this authority and to abide by the laws governing its control.

"I am sure you of all people, Mr Forester, will also appreciate that the business of removing the remains needs to take place as quickly as possible, that the new mine can be brought back into production and the workforce return. With this in mind, I do accept that it was the Home Office that initially dragged its feet – not of my doing I might add – resulting in the already considerable delay.

"If I was to put forward your appeal for time to call a public meeting with a view to the people of Pentrebach, somehow playing a part in the final resting place of the lost miners; this would create a further delay and might necessitate a decision on where to store the miners' remains until an agreement is achieved.

"Are you, Mr Forester, aware of a suitable facility in this vicinity that could accommodate such an arrangement?"

"With regard to a public meeting, Doctor Carmichael, I am confident that this could be arranged in a very short time; no, I do not, off hand, know of a place where the remains might be safely stored but I can assure you that if there is such a place I will very quickly find it."

So far the meeting had been dominated by just two men: Doctor Carmichael, and Max Forester. Now, however, Ken Gregory the National Coal Board's Agent motioned that he wished to speak. Collin Wright indicated that he should be allowed to do so.

"Gentlemen, I have listened with interest and understanding to Mr Forester's appeal and accept his compassionate reasoning behind it. However I must emphasize the point made by Doctor Carmichael that this unfortunate business has already resulted in the mine being shut down for several weeks, at a great loss to both the NCB and the miners. Mr Forester will be well aware that the NCB was not able to extend its earlier commitment to pay the miners a Day Wage income. I'm sure, therefore, that he will agree that any further avoidable delay may not go down well even with the rank and file; the very people from whom he will be seeking support for his idea."

"If I may," Forester began. "As I see it, Doctor Carmichael will need at least a few days to get back to London, meet with the appropriate people to discuss the matter and arrange his return accompanied by the appointed specialists. During this period I am convinced I can arrange a public meeting and learn whether my suggestion is favourable or not. I firmly believe that the villagers will not just agree but will be delighted to be involved in choosing the final resting place for the lost miners.

"Of course, I agree that getting everyone back to work is our number one priority and providing everything is acceptable to the villagers and a suitable place to store the remains is quickly obtained, there need be no further delay in a return to work. It really won't matter if arrangements for the placement of the remains takes time as long as the storage problem is overcome."

By now, although it was not expressed by anyone, it wasn't difficult to detect an air of general approval of Max Forester's plan; a low murmuring among the gathering illustrated a mood of assent. It was Doctor Carmichael who spoke above the muttering.

"Mr Forester, while I cannot guarantee Home Office approval of your plan, I want you to know that I will not personally impede it in any way. I will put your idea forward and explain as best I can the reasoning behind it. But the ball will be in your court, Mr Forester. Unless you can get the Pentrebach villagers to approve and locate a suitable place to accommodate the twenty-five miners' remains, within, let's say a week; the official procedure will go ahead and the remains removed and taken from this locality to a place designated by the Home Office; the matter will be entirely out of my and your hands."

"Thank you very much Doctor, if you will be so kind as to leave me a phone number where I can reach you I will let you know, as quickly as I can, if I have been able to achieve both aims."

"That will not be necessary Mr Forester, as soon as I have consulted with the Home Office I will phone you and let you know the outcome; I must emphasize however, that in the event of you not getting a favourable Home Office response, there will be little chance of changing it, especially given the limited time we have"

"I understand Doctor but by then the villagers will be aware of events and I will be guided by them.

With this the manager rose and brought the meeting to a close.

16

Max Forester was well aware of the enormous task he had set himself. His first port of call was the Aber-Afon-Gwen Town Council offices, for he would need the town council's approval to call a public meeting at Pentrebach. He did not relish this visit, especially as it would mean bringing Councillor Ben Collins, not his favourite person, in on the business.

Ironically, it was to Ben Collins' office that the desk clerk directed him. He tapped the door tentatively, anxious that his reception might not be a welcome one.

"Well, well, Mr Forester, to what do I owe this impromptu visit?"

"I have come here seeking your help Councillor Collins and if you will hear me out, I will explain why I need yours, or rather the Council's help and I am sure you will find that what I have come about is worthy of assistance. In saying this, I ask that for the sake of the delicate nature of my task, we set aside our past differences and consider only the matter under discussion."

"Very well, Mr Forester, I am prepared to listen to your request for help but, will reserve my judgement until I hear what you have to say."

So Forester began to relate the whole sequence of events from the finding of the Fault and as a consequence the revelation of the old Pentrebach Level leading to the discovery of the remains of the lost miners.

Councillor Collins listened with keen attention, interrupting just once briefly, to exclaim his astonishment at the discovery of the poor lost miners of that tragic accident. Then Forester came to the real reason for his visit, explaining that he needed to call a public meeting in Pentrebach, as it was he who put it to the Home Office representatives that the custody (not disposal) of the miners' remains should involve the Pentrebach villagers and not be left to a government department. He then went on to relate what Doctor Carmichael had said concerning the need for the earliest removal of the miners' remains and, if they were to be retained here, a suitable place of accommodation must be found very quickly. He concluded by expressing the Doctor's insistence that any decision would come from the Home Office and not himself, though he was prepared to put the Pentrebach case before the appropriate authority as convincingly as he could.

Ben Collins' response took Forester completely by surprise; not the usual challenging attitude which he had been accustomed to but an entirely supportive and friendly one.

"What you have just told me Max," the Councillor began, "is truly amazing. The Pentrebach tragedy has cast a cloud over, not only Pentrebach, but this entire valley for over ninety years. To have accidently hit upon the mine and discovered the remains of those poor lost miners will bring a great deal of relief and comfort to us all, for even though the subject is one of sadness and grief, its discovery can actually be said to be serendipitous. I am so glad you took it upon yourself to challenge the Home Office visitors on how the custody of the miners' remains should be handled. Max, you have done us all proud and I applaud you for it; what an awful thing it would have been if, as they suggested, the process had been carried out in secret. I can only imagine the later disappointment of the villagers.

"What I'd like you to do now, Max, if you will, is to return to the village and organise a meeting as quickly as you can; I will settle the matter with the other councillors who I am certain will support you all the way. In the meantime, as I have no doubt the villagers will also give you their full backing; I will be grateful if I am allowed to attend the meeting if only in a passive role. Well done Max! As for a place of storage though, I would suggest you seek somewhere in Pentrebach as the town might prove too far away for convenience.

This sudden flush of unprepared for total agreement, support and willingness to do all he could, on the part of the Councillor, had left Forester in a dazed state of elation. "I can't believe it, he even called me Max." He said to himself as he departed from the Civic Building.

It didn't take long for Forester to arrange a public meeting in the Pentrebach Miners' Welfare Hall. News of the discovery of the old Pentrebach Level and the remains of the lost miners quickly spread throughout the village ensuring a good turnout. The meeting was to take place in the evening of the next day. However, upon returning from his visit to the Town Civic Buildings with Ben Collins, Forester arrived back at the NUM office just in time to receive a phone call from the colliery manager asking him to attend the colliery site office, where he had something to show him, along with some other gentlemen he had also invited. As he journeyed up to the colliery, Forester wondered what the manager could possibly want; he sincerely hoped it would not interfere with any of his plans.

At the manager's office were: Ken Gregory, Collin Wright and Walter Francis and Foresters' own second-in-command, Frank Lewis.

"Well Frank, I didn't expect to see you here" Forester remarked as he entered the room.

"I was in the house when Mr Wright phoned and he told me he had already phone you"

"Oh, that explains it then."

When they were all seated the manager began.

"Gentlemen, thank you for attending at such short notice but I have only just learned something of considerable interest and most revealing. You may recall Doctor Carmichael handing me a package as we were leaving the site of the old Level. Well, what he handed me has proven to be something quite special. It was wrapped in a piece of old moleskin, much dilapidated now, which must have been cut from the owner's trousers, moleskin trousers were quite common in those days. It had been held together with shot wire. Underneath was a Shotsmans' leather-bound duty book, in which he would record any holes he fired or, as he would have also acted as Deputy, anything relevant to each day's working for one week, fortunately it was a Monday so he had a clean book. These books had blank sheets every other and it is on these blank sheets that this Shotsman wrote an account of events leading up to the explosion and afterwards, while, in fact he, like the others, lay there trapped and helpless. It's obviously due to the care he took to make it secure that the note book is so well preserved; despite it having been submerged in water for all that time. With your permission, I will read it to you rather than pass it around for each of you to read in turn. You will appreciate its delicate condition and our desire to preserve it.

There was a general nod of approval, so the manager began:

"Clive Harding – Deputy/Shotsman

Monday 14th January 1863:

At the end of this our first day confined as we are, I have begun to use this note book to recount the day's events and beyond if necessary.

Before I entered the mine this morning I witnessed a heated debate between the colliers and Steve Parfitt the colliery Overman. They were standing just outside the mine portal. The issue was an ongoing one over the poor air quality at the coalface. The men were annoyed that after many attempts to get the Owners to begin work on a Return Airway or Shaft nothing had been done. Even though the Overman assured them that work on the Airway was to start soon, as such promises had been made several times before, they demanded that they get confirmation from a Company official or representative today or they may consider withdrawing their labour in the near future.

This will be a drastic move on their part as such action would leave them out of work with no income. Pentrebach Level is in its early days with only seventeen colliers and four boys employed on the coalface. The Company has another three, more productive mines on Squire Watkins Estate lands alone, so will not be put under any serious pressure from a walk out at this mine; especially as it couldn't possibly last very long.

Anyway, Eddie Jones – the other Shotsman – and I decided to go on ahead and left the debate for them to settle. We were joined by Ivor Williams and Bill Evans – the Alliars- who were leading the four cobs in. On the way in we met Sam Thorn the Repairer who was just taking his tools off the bar; we exchanged greetings and passed on.

It was some time before the colliers joined us at the coalface. When they arrived I spoke to Tom Bishop, who had been the spokesman at the meeting and he told me that they had put enough pressure on the Overman to ensure that he would get in touch with Leslie Eaton, General Manager or even Peter Driscoll, Mining Engineer sometime today. He told me that he had suggested that at the very least a larger fan could be installed to get the air moving again. He believed that the recent Fault the coal face had met, which had changed the direction of the mine, might well be the reason for the present poor air flow. Whatever, he confirmed that if they do not have any positive response by the end of the week, the men really will walk off the colliery site in protest.

Eventually the colliers got down to work and it wasn't long before the sixth dram, making the first complete journey was being taken out to the double parting by Ivor Williams and the white cob.

Work went on in the stalls when after about fifteen minutes we heard a distant loud bang followed by a strong gush of air pushing against us. Everyone was alarmed and so when I said I'd go back to see what has happened there was no stopping the rest of them from following me. When we arrived above the double parting there was no sign of the journey or Ivor Williams. For the journey to have gone, Sam the Repairer must have coupled the last dram and signalled the winding house to haul the journey out. The white cob stood alone tethered to a post.

There was nothing left to do but to walk on up the drift to find out what had happened.

Sam and Ivor were standing next to what was the last dram of the journey. Eddie and I, as Deputies, moved up to where we could see that the third dram, only half of which was visible, had a wheel lodged between a gap in the rails. Beyond this were some large loose boulders in front of a solid wall of rock. We determined that there had been an explosion and that in every probability the cause had been the ignition of a pocket of gas from sparks created by the revolution of the metal wheel in the gap between the rails. I surmised that the after damp, which would have left us in an atmosphere of carbon monoxide, must have travelled outwards towards the portal, for which we must be grateful.

I called Sam over and asked him what he thought of it when he, quite without prompting, confessed that he had been working in that very spot earlier and had joined the two rails together as a gap had developed.

I must admit I lost my temper with him; pointing out that he should not have tackled such a job on his own. I told him that it was a two man job and that the rails should have been taken up and realigned. He, however, rightly pointed out that it wasn't unusual for rail joints to part and that he could not have foreseen the explosion. He said he had done this job himself many times in the past; it never being easy to get help when he needed it. Besides he wanted to get the job done quickly because the colliers had already lost a lot of time this morning due to the dispute.

It was Tom Bishop who brought us down to earth when he said that this was not the time to be looking to blame anyone.

"The most important thing now is to consider how we are going to get out of here."

Tom Bishop was right of course and upon reflection, I told Sam that I appreciated that he was only trying to act in the best interests of the men and could not have anticipated or even thought about a gas explosion; no one was blaming him for our predicament.

Having settled down I took charge and asked a few of the men to go back to the coalface for some tools: shovels, mandrels and sledges to help breakup and remove some of the debris that confronted us. While they were away I asked for silence and with a large stone began tapping the two pipes –water and air- to see if we could get any response from the outside but there was nothing. Not to add to their despair I pointed out that the reason we had no response might be down to the pipes being flattened and thereby no sound could travel through them from either end.

When the men returned with the tools, at my suggestion we worked four men, two either side of the last dram, at fifteen minute intervals, in order not to over exert. However, after several hours we found we were making very little progress, having only removed the loose boulders and made no impression upon the rock face. It was decided that it made more sense to abandon our efforts and leave it to those on the outside who were better equipped.

I had already arranged that we pool our water and food, that an organised rationing system can be made. Fortunately, the explosion occurred before the break for food. I have also arranged the lighting in order to save oil and candles; using just two tallow lights for comfort and my oil wick lamp to enable me to write these notes.

The four ponies have been brought up to just above the double parting and along with the one already there, have been tethered to individual posts with sufficient rein to eat from their nose bags or lie down if they wish; this is all we can do for them.

Sam and I are the only ones who have a watch, so we have coordinated them and will keep them both fully wound as time will soon mean nothing under here. I told the men that if we are still here by mid-night I will mark a cross on a nearby post so that we can note the passing of one day into the next.

I have tried to comfort the younger boys with assurances that the rescue team will be with us soon. The youngest lad has already had a moment of panic and alarm. However, as the last few hours have witnessed no sign of any imminent help, there is little else I can say by way of encouragement.

We are all just sitting or lying down to wait, there really is nothing else we can do. At midnight I marked an X on the post - end of day one. What will tomorrow bring.

Tuesday 15th January

Today, around mid-day Andrew Lloyd suggested that we should at least try and have another go at the rock. While I didn't challenge the idea I had serious doubts of any success. However, before we could put the matter to a vote young Ken Jones interrupted wanting to know why we shotsmen had not attempted to blast our way out.

It occurred to me that I had overlooked the fact that the young lads would not be aware of the futility of such an attempt, so I explained that the powder we use was unlikely to have much effect upon the rock and if we did attempt to fire, we could cause another explosion and besides that, the smoke from the firing would only make the already poor air quality worse. Of course the older men were already aware of this but I felt happier now that I had enlightened the younger ones.

Poor young Ken Jones, who must have thought he had come up with the answer to our liberty, walked away with head bent low; I wanted to comfort him but left it to his father; there was little I could say that might help.

A vote was cast and it was agreed to try once again to break through the rock. However, after many hours of serious effort on the part of us all, it was truly apparent that we were wasting our time and energy. After we had agreed to give it up I pointed out that there was nothing wrong with Andrew's suggestion but we must all now accept that we are left to depend on those from the outside.

Midnight and another X on the post - end of day two.

Wednesday 16th

Tom Bishop and I spend most of the time talking and, as with the rest, sometimes involuntarily sleeping. Today we discussed the Fault the mine had hit some time ago which had caused the coalface to veer to the right and several weeks delay in production. Tom, who was convinced that this had also affected the air quality, wondered if I thought the lost production had brought about a further delay in the cutting of the much debated Return Air Way or Shaft. I told him that I believed it undoubtedly did, as the Company was not about to waste money on a further non-productive operation so soon after the unforeseen delay.

Tom's son Ben is in a distressed state and keeps asking his father of the chances of our being rescued. After telling him that there was nothing else we can do this end Tom tried to offer some assurance of a breakthrough but the lad is old enough to realise that hope is getting ever less likely. I was particularly affected when Ben told his father

"I don't know how to die Dad." Who does, I wonder?

Sid Llewellyn, however, did try to inspire the boy into believing there was still hope of getting out. Ben is courting Sid's daughter and Sid spoke of his and his wife's delight at the prospect of their marriage. I'm not sure if Ben felt comforted by this or even more distraught; contemplating, that his future is more likely to end in here.

With no sound or evidence of any rescue team, Tom and I and I suspect most of the others, are convinced that there is going to be no rescue; it is becoming ever more apparent that the fall must extend too far to penetrate;

Another X on the post at midnight, as we reach the end of day three.

Thursday 17th

Food and water are running seriously low. This morning I persuaded Tom bishop to join me to go and see how far the water level had risen. We took two Jacks with us to carry some water back; though of course it can only be drunk as a last resort as it will not be healthy stuff. We also took two oil-wick lights, leaving the remaining tallow candles for the comfort of the others. We soon realised that it was going to be as much as we could manage just to stand up. We both felt drained of energy and the air was quite oppressive. The water had already completely covered the work area and was making its way up to the double parting. Just above which the four ponies were tethered. We wondered how long it will be before they are overcome by the water but we dare not release them, for fear of their running wild. We were so weak it took us quite some time to get back.

Upon our return we explained the circumstances to those who were awake – many now were sleeping almost all the time – telling them exactly what we had seen but still encouraging them to not give up. However, in response to this, one of the boys shouted out, "Shut up! And stop pretending there is any chance of us getting out of here." We said no more.

After a long silence three young lads; Fred Lloyd and the brothers Ken and Brian Jones, suddenly rose up and in a wild and frenzied moment, picked up their mandrels and rushed to the blockage fiercely lashing out at the rock face, creating a fountain of sparks filling the air. There was nothing we could physically do to restrain them for fear of being injured by the flailing mandrels. With the remaining two tallow candles almost down to their last, there was little light to see them, so any attempt to interrupt the young lads would have been most precarious. However, just as suddenly as they had started so they ceased; falling to the ground each in a state of exhaustion and despair.

One of the colliers from behind me accused them of risking all our lives, had they caused another explosion.

Ken Jones' tearful and remarkable reply adequately expressed their feelings:

"What do you think we were trying to do; better that than waiting for death to creep up on us i'nit?" – He screamed -or words to that effect.

This must have hit home as no one offered a response.

Not long after this unfortunate outburst by the young lads, we felt a tremor and a little later two more. We were convinced it was an attempt by the outside crew to blast their way in with dynamite; whether or not this was the case, all too soon it went quiet again, as if confirming the futility of their efforts.

As the day comes to a close the silence is once again broken when a mixture of loud hideous screeching mixed with choking-gurgling sounds can be heard; clear evidence of the cobs' final struggle against the inevitable rise of the water.

One lad shouted out "The ponies are drowning, the ponies are drowning." And in a much weaker voice it sounded as if the said, "we're next."

The silence that has ensued since is perhaps more terror-provoking than the cob's final battle.

Fear and fatigue are now our greatest enemies as we near another midnight. Not just boys but grown men are now openly afraid. We have heard so much of the heroism of miners in similar circumstances of the past; but I and I know those about me, do not feel much like heroes at this desperate time. I have decided not to write any more as I, along with the others, keep falling into a deep sleep and I want to try to secure my note book before I am completely overcome. I cannot get up to mark the X this time.

"God help us."

"Good God," Forester gasped. "That is quite a document, Mr Wright. What an incredibly brave man this Clive Harding must have been."

"It is indeed a remarkable document, Max, and it is also an invaluable one; there will now be no need to carry out an inspection of the site of the explosion, Mr Harding has explained fully what took place. His heartrending story ends with him and the others bereft of energy, food and water but above all, hope. There just was no way they were ever going to get out of that mine. What a terrible time it must have been for them and for all those relatives and friends outside unable to help them. This gives so much more support to your bid Max, to get them out and lay them to rest here in Pentrebach, I'm sure you can rely upon the NCB to back you all the way. "

17

The next day, the day of the meeting, Forester was delighted to receive a phone call from Doctor Carmichael; it came at three o'clock in the afternoon.

"Mr Forester, Doctor Carmichael here. Do you have some positive news for me regarding the village meeting and the availability of a place to store the miners' remains?"

"Yes, I do, Doctor, at least in part, but more importantly sir, has the Home Office agreed to my request?"

"The Home Office has agreed that providing the miners' remains can be removed individually and conveyed safely to a storage location acceptable to me and my team, they are prepared to hand the business of disposal – and I apologise for the term – over to the jurisdiction of whatever Official Council Body the village of Pentrebach comes under. Is this a satisfactory result for you Mr Forester?"

"Indeed it is Doctor Carmichael, for I have already consulted with the Aber-Afon-Gwen Council and they are as anxious as I am that the village and indeed the entire valley should be left to determine the last resting place of those poor miners lost in the Pentrebach disaster. Unfortunately, as yet I have not been able to secure a storage place for the remains but I am hopeful that at the public meeting, scheduled for tonight, someone will come forward with a suitable location."

Forester went on to tell the Doctor what the package he handed to Mr Wright, when leaving the site of the old Pentrebach Level, contained. The Doctor expressed his astonishment and delight at such a discovery.

"What an incredible revelation this must be to you and the colliery management; it obviously dispenses with the need to investigate the cause of the accident and, although tragically, helps to better understand the circumstances those poor souls found themselves in."

"Everything suggests Mr Forester that your proposal is a most worthy one and I wish you well in your endeavours. Let us hope that you are successful in obtaining a suitable place to retain the miners' remains at tonight's meeting."

The Doctor confirmed that he and the team would be arriving in three days' time and that in the meantime he will contact Mr Wright, that he might make preparations for them to visit the location of the old mine and provision for the removal and conveyance of the remains to the surface of the colliery. He explained that they would be bringing a specially adapted vehicle, capable of carry seven stretchers, which will mean that it will require four journeys; three if seven and one of four, to the storage room wherever it may be, unless additional suitable vehicles can be found.

"I would suggest a place not too far from the colliery for convenience sake." The Doctor concluded.

"I'll do my best Doctor." Forester confirmed. "I am most obliged to you."

Later on Forester phoned Ben Collins and told him that the meeting had been arranged for six o'clock at the Miners' Welfare Hall. He also told him of Clive Harding's note book and that the Home Office was happy to allow the people to take care of the miners' remains providing the Council was involved and a suitable temporary storage place could be found by the time the Doctor and his team arrive, in three days. He assured the Councillor that he would be more than welcome to join him on the stage at the meeting and express anything he might feel by way of a contribution to the proceedings.

Councillor Collins could barely take it all in. The note book, he was sure, would form an important part of the history of that tragic day and retain its place for posterity. That the Home Office had consented to allow the people along with the Council to secure the permanent resting place for the miners; who will no longer be considered "lost," was excellent news. He felt a place in the village of Pentrebach to store the "bodies" would be better than "here in Aber-Afon-Gwen" but if one could not be found he would make every endeavour to locate one in the town.

"I am grateful to you Max for granting me a voice at your meeting; I can assure you that I will do all I can to promote your efforts and promise the people the full support on behalf of the council when, as I'm sure you will, need help towards the cost of obtaining a location for the burials and the burials themselves. Upon this matter I have already spoken to the other councillors all of whom endorse this commitment."

"Well, Mr Collins," Forester was about to begin,

"Ben, Max please, let's not stand on ceremony anymore, the nature of these events calls for a more compatible relationship."

"I can't thank you enough, Ben. Yes, of course there will be much to sort out and funding will play a very important part of it. It is my intention, once the village has given its approval, of which I am totally optimistic, to call upon them to help set up a Fund 'In aid of the Old Pentrebach Level miners' final resting place' if that is not too protracted a title."

"That's a perfectly appropriate title Max, and I'm convinced it will get overwhelming support and contributions. I look forward to seeing you at the Meeting tonight, all the best 'til then.

When the councillor put down the phone Max felt delighted with a perfect day and confident of a just as perfect evening to come.

The Meeting

Once again, as with the meeting to decide the outcome of the new mine, Pentrebach Miners' Welfare Hall appeared inadequate to cater for the throng now occupying every available inch of space, in a determined effort to gain admission. But this was going to be a different kind of meeting; the audience would not consist of people with opposing views on the topic under discussion. No, they will be of one voice; especially after hearing what Max Forester has to say concerning the recent discovery of the old Pentrebach Level workings.

Something else did not reflect the setting of the earlier meeting either. Where there had been ten people on the stage, tonight there would be just two: Max Forester and Councillor Ben Collins. A less likely partnership it would be difficult – in past times – to imagine. Two men known to be constant antagonists were now chatting genially and exchanging pleasantries as would two long established friends.

When everyone had settled in, not all as comfortably as they would wish, but nonetheless attentively, Max Forester rose and thanked everyone for being present and apologised for the unfortunate lack of accommodation.

"Ladies and gentlemen, I have called this public meeting to bring you news of the recent chance discovery of the old Pentrebach Level and as a consequence the sad remains of those unfortunate miners who have remained out of reach for over ninety years.

"Before I begin I would like to thank Councillor Ben Collins here, for his and the Councils' total support and co-operation in helping me put forward my proposition. It's no secret that Councillor Collins and I have, on numerous occasions crossed lances, but after a very congenial meeting we have agreed to put the past to bed and are now working in harmony in dealing with this most important issue. Councillor Collins will address the meeting after I have finished.

"What I have to say will be detailed and informative, because I want every man and woman in this valley to know exactly what happened and what I and many others already aware, believe should now take place. I ask only that you bear with me while I relate the events that have led to the reason for this meeting.

"Some time ago the colliers working in the new mine, discovered that the coalface was taking on an unusual colour. The coal started to show blue and gold strands throughout, which they were unable to explain. The matter was brought to the attention of the manager and he called upon the services of the NCB geologist Mr Jeffrey Maddocks. Mr Maddocks informed the manager that the discolouration of the coal was caused by water but not that commonly found in 'wet coalfaces' this was pressurised water from behind the coal.

"This, Mr Maddocks pointed out, might suggest the presence of an unrecorded mine –usually Victorian- crossing the path of the current operations. When questioned about this Mr Wright said that the only mine he knew of anywhere near was the old Pentrebach Level but as he, the geologist, was well aware, the NCB had purposely avoided any contact with that mine.

"It was decided to continue to bore five feet ahead daily, before any cutting and should any water come through the bore hole, they would take steps to pump it out. When water did start to come through, this is what they did. The mine was closed while this operation took place, which lasted about a week. When the water stopped flowing they cut their way through the coal to find an open space with a dramroad running in front of them. You can imagine their surprise at this discovery. To the right, at the end of the dramroad were a series of pillar and stall workings –for those not acquainted with this term- this was an early method of working the coal, where usually two men or one man and a boy worked in each stall. They found that there were a few half-filled drams but no tools. This suggested that the men had left in a hurry and taken their tools with them. Tools at the end of a shift would have been left nearby on each collier's bar, passed through a hole in the handles with a lock attached for safe keeping.

"But there was something else that struck them as peculiar. The coalface had earlier taken a diversion to the right as a result of a Fault. Mr Maddocks explained that this was a particular type of Fault called a Balk Fault. He pointed out that sometimes a Fault can result in the complete loss of a coalface, but in this case the seam instead of running in a straight horizontal course had been shifted by this geological disturbance. I'm sorry if this all sounds a bit complicated but as it is the reason the new mine came into contact with the old Pentrebach Level, it is important that you are made aware that this could not possibly have been anticipated by the NCB.

"When the men followed the dramroad back from the coalface, already suspicious that this could be the old Pentrebach Level, their suspicions were confirmed when they came across the skeletons of four ponies and further on the lost miners. Mr Wright immediately abandoned the investigation and they returned to the surface where he got in touch with the NCB officials who, in turn, got in touch with the Home Office, which is obligatory under such circumstances.

"I was part of the group that made the second visit to the old Pentrebach Level and so were three representatives of the Home Office including the Chief Medical Officer, Doctor Carmichael. When we arrived at the scene of the miners' remains and the Doctor and his colleagues had carried out their inspection; based on the circumstances shown and the body count it was agreed and confirmed that this was indeed the old Pentrebach Level. Out of respect we observed a minute's silence.

"Before we left Doctor Carmichael told us that the removal of the remains will be carried out by qualified Home Office appointed men, of which he would be one and that the process would be done in secret, with only a few officials from the NCB, NUM and a small party of selected labourers along with his team, present. He also said that after the miners' remains were removed from the mine, they would be taken to an appropriate place for disposal. I was not happy with this and despite having assured the manager that I would not interfere with the proceedings while the Home Office people were there; I felt I had to speak out.

"I told the doctor that I felt, far from being kept secret, the entire population of the village should be made aware of this discovery and should be given the opportunity to at least play a part in deciding and arranging the last resting place of these poor souls.

At that moment Forester paused and apologised for the length of time this matter was taking to explain but emphasized that he wanted to be sure they had the full story.

"Thank you for being so patient I will try to keep the rest of the business as brief as I can."

"Back at the office both the manager and I spoke of the disaster, Mr Wright dealing in detail with the series of events and me adding that the village of Pentrebach had carried the heavy burden of the failure to rescue any of the men or even to retrieve a single body for over ninety years; and that this was now an opportunity to, in some way, relieve that burden.

"After listening with genuine interest and understanding, Doctor Carmichael said that he could now understand how such sentiment could be aroused over the issue and he agreed to put the case for the villagers to have a say in the removal and custody of the miners' remains to the Home Office authorities.

"However, Doctor Carmichael did express that even if the Home Office agrees to my proposals there will be conditions. The remains will have to be brought out of the mine by trained appointed government people and if they are not to be taken away immediately a suitable and approved building will have to be found to store them, in the meantime. The overriding issue is time. Earlier today Doctor Carmichael phoned me to confirm that the Home Office has agreed to the proposals providing the Aber-Afon-Gwen Council is involved and the conditions put to me by the Doctor are adhered to. Councillor Collins assured me that the Council are only too pleased to get involved. However, we have just three days before the Doctor and his team arrive, which means we must find a suitable place for the remains to be stored before that. Time is also important because there has been enough delay in production and of course loss of men's wages.

"Before I hand over to Councillor Collins, there is something else which I must refer to." Forester exclaimed. "When we were leaving the mine after the inspection, Doctor Carmichael handed the manger a package he had picked up near one of the miners' bodies. This package, wrapped in a leather case and moleskin cover, had survived in relatively good condition and proved to be very significant. It is a Deputy/shotsman's note book owned by a man called Clive Harding, in which he wrote an account of the explosion and a daily account of how the men survived thereafter, up to the time he became too weak to continue. This is a most remarkable document and has enlightened us of the events of this tragedy immeasurably. What this man did under such terrible circumstances is a testimony to his courage and control. I'm sure it will be placed in a safe location for posterity and its contents published and made available to a wider public.

"Gratefully, I have been permitted to bring the document here tonight to read to you; I regret that I cannot allow anyone to handle it in view of its importance and its fragile condition. Before I begin I want to emphasize that this tragedy occurred in the Victorian era and therefore it was Victorian standards of life and business that applied. I stress this because, only if you consider the time and practices of the period will you appreciate that what might not be acceptable today was perfectly normal at that time. It is therefore important not to judge, what you may consider wrong or unacceptable in the case of certain people's actions at the time; it would be a gross mistake to look to blame anyone, based upon our contemporary interpretation of right and wrong.

Forester had taken this precaution because of the absence of the Return Airway or Shaft and the actions of Sam Thorn, with regard to the gap in the rails; all too aware that the Reverend Samuel Thorn, a descendent, was in the audience. He was determined that nothing was going to detract from this moment of Pentrebach's elation; at having discovered and retrieved the lost miners.

With that he read Clive Harding's notes slowly and with the warmth that they deserved. There was in response a standing ovation; and no one made any adverse comment.

"In conclusion I want to emphasize that providing you agree to the project ahead of us and without your agreement there can be no project, there is much to be done. The immediate priority is of course finding a suitable place of storage and establishing a Fund 'In Aid of the Old Pentrebach Level Miners' Final Resting Place' as we will undoubtedly need a good sum of money. Can I therefore, ask you to raise your hands if you feel that it is we, the people of Pentrebach and surrounds who should take it upon ourselves to give these miners, no longer lost, a final resting place worthy of their sacrifice?"

The response was overwhelming; everyone in the room not only raised their hands but stood up and applauded Max Forester, cheering and chanting: "Well done Max, well done Max."

When the din had subsided Ben Collins rose to his feet and added:

"Ladies and gentlemen I cannot agree with you more, what Max has achieved here is monumental.

"There isn't a man or woman or indeed child in this valley, who is not familiar with the Pentrebach Level disaster. The story of this terrible tragedy has always been a personal one for this area. There have been other mining disasters throughout this coalfield but this one was different, unique in fact, for not only were no lives saved but not one single body recovered. And Max is quite right when he says it was the failure to bring anyone out of the mine that has caused the greatest and longest lasting pain and burden. Now, at long last, there is an opportunity to ease that burden at least to some extent, by creating a resting place for all twenty-five victims in a recognised, permanent sacred place.

"I want you to know that the Council is giving its full support to this project as I have already raised the matter with my colleagues who are fully committed so to do. We will also approach the NCB to see if they will help and I am quietly confident of success there to. There remains, as Max explained the matter of a place of storage. I have spoken to Max on the subject and he agrees with me that it would be best if such a location can be found in Pentrebach village rather than Aber-Afon-Gwen, but I am sure that if this cannot be achieved I will be able to find somewhere appropriate in the town."

In response to this a man in the audience rose and asked if he be allowed to speak. Collins nodded his approval and Forester responded with:

"We welcome anyone's comments sir, and will be glad to listen to whatever you have to say.

"Gentlemen, my name is Bernard Carter and I am the Minister of Bethel Chapel, here in Pentrebach, which I am sure you are acquainted with. I may be able to help you with the storage space for the miners' remains, providing the chapel Deacons and members agree. About two years ago we had erected a hall on land in the new housing site, which we use for functions such as jumble sales, tea-parties Christmas plays, etc. It is a spacious and very secure building and will easily accommodate your needs. I will however, need to hold a meeting with the Deacons and members to find out how they feel about it as it must be a collective decision, but providing there is nothing of any special significance that the hall is due to be used for, I feel sure they will be only too happy to help you out."

"Minister Carter," Forester responded, "this could well be the answer to our prayers. Of course you must first consult those involved in the chapel's affairs and should they wish to speak to me independently I will be more than happy to meet with them. I cannot thank you enough for being prepared to approach them and I look forward to their decision.

"However, there is the question of time; as I pointed out earlier we only have a couple of days to find a suitable place. So in the event that you are unable to arrange a meeting of the Deacons and members quickly enough, as an added precaution I will call upon Councillor Collins to go ahead and seek a place in the town. But if in the meantime you have been successful and everyone at the chapel is happy, it will be to our advantage to accept your kind offer of a place in the village and I'm sure Councillor Collins will have no difficulty in cancelling any alternative arrangement he may have made. Is that suitable to you Minister?

"Certainly, Mr Forester and I will make every endeavour to get back to you with an answer as soon as I can."

Councillor Collins stood to acknowledge his agreement with Forester's suggestions.

To add to this very good prospect, a group of women had got together and approached Forester. They told him that they would create a Fund committee 'In Aid of the Old Penterbach Level Miners' Final Resting Place' and would set about organising themselves the very next day. They were the members of the local Women's

Institute and were quite practiced in this field; fundraising being a very significant part of their structure.

Forester could not have wished for a more successful meeting. He left the Welfare Hall talking to Councillor Collins in a mood of joy and elation.

"It could not have gone better Ben, I am confident that we have overcome the first stage in our endeavour to see these miners are laid to rest at last. The big question as I see it now is; where are we going to put them to rest?"

"Let's take each step at a time Max, as you say, tonight has been particularly successful and as long as we have the storage facility, be it mine or the Ministers', we will have time on our hands for a change. Once again Max you have done extraordinarily well and I congratulate you."

"I certainly didn't do it alone Ben, and besides there is still an awful lot to do and I'm going to need all the help I can get; and yours and the Council's support will be vital. I would like to thank you for your kind words in there and your intention to consult the NCB for its support also. I believe if we work in tandem this story can have a truly satisfying ending. That the ladies of the WI are taking on the responsibility for the Fund is another major step in the right direction; they are so adept at that sort of thing."

The two men parted in good spirits; perhaps for the first time.

18

Bernard Carter, Bethel Chapel Minister, had made a special effort by calling an emergency meeting of the chapel deacons and members the day immediately after the public meeting. They were all already aware of the Pentrebach Level issue of course, it being common knowledge throughout the village by now. Their response to granting the use of the Chapel Hall to store the miners' remains was positive; they were only too pleased to be playing a part in this momentous event.

The day of the Home Office team's arrival came and they were taken to the location of the Hall in order to gain it their approval; Forester and the Minister were both confident that it would meet with their demands.

"This will be quite suitable," Doctor Carmichael told Forester, and his colleagues added their words of agreement. After a brief chat with the Minister and a couple of Deacons, expressing their gratitude, the party, including Forester and Frank Lewis, left for the colliery site.

At the colliery they were met by Ben Collins and fellow Councillor Bryn Thomas, along with Collin Wright, Walter Francis and twelve colliers, including Oliver Hardwick and Desmond Richards.

Ben Collins and his colleague stayed only long enough to introduce themselves and to inform the Doctor that they will be present at Bethel Chapel Hall to ensure that things run smoothly that end. Ben Collins expressed his gratitude to the Doctor for helping to ensure that the miners' remains stay here in the valley where it is overwhelmingly felt they belong.

After the two councillors had departed, Collin Wright began to explain what the procedure would be, he having consulted with Doctor Carmichael over the phone beforehand.

"We have adapted a spake to provide a suitable carrier, by removing the seats and replacing them with flat boards with straps attached, to hold the remains on. For convenience sake the skeleton bodies will be sealed in specially designed body bags provided by the Home Office. They will be carried along the old mine to the carrier at the lower new mine, on individual stretchers. This of course will need to be done manually and with a great deal of care and caution given the uneven terrain along the old dram road.

"You twelve men will, in pairs, make two journeys to and from the spake. You will leave with a stretcher in equal intervals allowing space between stretchers for safety sake. There will be a need for two of you to make an extra trip to bring back the final body, making twenty-five in all.

"When we arrive at the scene of the human remains Doctor Carmichael and his colleagues will examine them and prepare each one for removal, then they will control the lifting of the remains, hopefully without any further damage, into the bags and onto the stretchers. If we all abide by the experts' instructions I'm sure things will go smoothly. Once we have loaded the stretchers onto the carrier –which is designed to carry all twenty-five – I will signal the haulage man and he will haul the carrier out very slowly; there will be enough room for us to sit alongside the stretchers. We will travel down on the carrier as it is fitted with collapsible handles for us to hold on to.

"As you can see, Gentlemen, there are four vehicles here which will carry the remains to the Chapel Hall in the village. The largest one is a Home Office vehicle capable of carrying seven stretchers, the others, belonging to the NCB Mines Rescue Service, can accommodate four each. Therefore, a single journey using all four vehicles will carry nineteen stretchers, which means that the Home Office vehicle will make a second journey for the remaining six. If everything is clear, Gentlemen, we will begin our task."

With that they made their way to the waiting specially adapted spake.

The removal of the miners' remains was carried out with no real problems; though it took some considerable time. It was the lifting and bagging of the fragile skeleton bodies in such a way as to cause the least damage, that was the greatest part of the task. Doctor Carmichael asked Forester if the intention was to bury the bodies individually or in a prepared mass grave. Forester explained that the former was his personal choice and he would make every effort to achieve that.

"As it is Doctor," Forester explained, "we have not determined a location, this will now be our priority and it is this that will also determine the nature of the burials. Personally, I will be very disappointed if, after all the time and effort to ensure these miners are removed and contained individually, we should lose the impact of our aim in having to resort to a communal grave."

"Knowing your determination Mr Forester, I am confident that you will succeed in your endeavours."

At Bethel Chapel Hall, as the vehicles arrived and the stretchers carefully carried in –watched by a crowd of village spectators- Councillor Ben Collins and his colleague, Councillor Bryn Thomas were anxious to officiate and Forester and the others obliged by following their instructions as to the order of an agreed layout.

When the Home Office vehicle arrived for the second time with the final six miners' remains, they were taken inside the hall and the door was closed. However, shortly afterwards the door opened again and the twelve volunteer colliers left, having completed their role and been thanked profusely for their services, at the same time the two colliery officials, Collin Wright and Walter Francis, also left.

It wasn't long before the door was once again opened when Doctor Carmichael and his team prepared to depart on their long journey. They were joined by Forester, Lewis and the two Councillors.

Forester and the two Councillors expressed their gratitude for all they had done in a most efficient and co-operative manner. Forester promised to let Doctor Carmichael know how the remaining act of bringing about a final recognised resting place for the Old Pentrebach Level Miners, plays out.

"I wish you every success Mr Forester, maybe I'll pay the site a visit myself someday. I have become so affected by this whole affair that it will be difficult for me not to."

"You will be more than welcome Doctor and once again many, many thanks."

And so the Home Office Team drove away and the three men went back into the hall.

"Well Max, it's done, Councillor Collins remarked. "The next move is down to us, by which I mean local people. The search is on for that burial site and I like you Max, am determined it will be a site worthy of those men and capable of catering for twenty-five graves, not one mass grave."

As they were talking the Minister of Bethel Chapel approached and asked Forester what steps were going to be taken to locate a burial place for the miners.

"Well first, Minister, I'd like to once again thank you and your deacons and members for the use of the hall, it has made things so much easier to have found a place in the village. As yet I'm afraid, with so much to do in organising the removal of the miners' remains; we have had no time to deliberate over this final duty.

Councillor Collins and his colleagues and a number of the village residents have agreed to assist me in this endeavour and we shall get together very soon to discuss the matter and hopefully not be too long in finding a suitable place. Of course, Minister, you will be kept up to date and will be the first person I shall contact when we are, as I'm sure we will be, successful."

19

The initial meeting to discuss finding and acquiring a suitable site for the final resting place of the Old Pentrebach Level Miners, was convened in the NUM Office in Pentrebach village; where ordinarily Max Forester and Frank Lewis, along with their NUM committee members, would conduct their business. The building formed a prefabricated extension to the Miners' Welfare Hall.

The room was laid out with a large table at the far end with a row of tables leading off from the centre, a step lower. There were six chairs behind the large table; seating for the NUM officials at their meetings and twelve chairs either side of the centre row, which would ordinarily cater for the other committee members. Against the walls along both sides of the room were filing cabinets and cupboards with more chairs interspersed, over which were photographs of leading NUM figures of the past and relevant NUM notices.

On this occasion those occupying four of the higher seats were, Max Forester, Frank Lewis Councillor Ben Collins and Councillor Bryn Thomas. Seated, five either side, along the centre row were ten village residents, three of whom were women, who had volunteered to assist in the task at hand.

Forester opened the meeting thus:

"Good evening ladies and gentlemen. The business we are about to discuss is already well known to you but it is nonetheless a very important part of the collective effort in taking custody of, and securing a place for, the lost miners' of Pentrebach Level. The search is on for a final resting place of dignity and perpetual recognition; that future generations will be able to visit a unique memorial site, which will help them understand why the people of their village took so much pride in establishing it."

"There is no common land in the neighbourhood of the village and we have already established that where there are open fields, every one of them, understandably, is owned and used by someone. The parish church graveyard is only used for the burial of family members with graves occupied by earlier deceased relatives no new graves have been opened in many years; besides there would be nowhere near enough room within the precincts of the churchyard for our needs. If anyone here is aware of a suitable plot of land that might be negotiated for, please tell us now that we might make appropriate inquiries?"

Tom Chambers, who owned a grocers shop in the village, pointed out that most of the now few farmers left in the area, use their fields for sheep grazing alternating with hay harvesting.

"Perhaps we could persuade one of them to allocate a plot big enough for our purpose in a remote part of their land?" He suggested.

Councillor Collins rose to reply.

"I attended a meeting of farmers in the town hall recently; this was a meeting of farmers from many areas, including our valley. I wasn't able to address the meeting but afterwards I spoke to our local farmers, who explained that even if they could afford to give up some land for the burial site, their fields are governed by a strict law to only be used for agricultural purpose. While I feel that we might be able to approach the government on this matter; I didn't detect much enthusiasm for the idea from the farmers."

Max Forester suggested that they put an advert in the local press for a suitable plot of land; not necessarily a field, to see if any offers come forth. This was agreed but it would seem that no one could come up with any other hopeful suggestions and the meeting lost its impact.

Max Forester called for everyone present to make it known throughout the village what we are seeking and how important it is to find something soon.

"If we do fail to find a place, we will have no alternative other than to recall the Home Office to take the miners' remains away. After all we have done to keep them here where they unquestionably belong, I know that I personally will be devastated and I'm sure my feelings are shared, not only by you here tonight, but by the whole village. We must find an appropriate location and we must find it soon. What does give us a slight advantage is that unlike cemeteries, which are, whenever possible, sited in ground which is conducive to decomposition; our poor souls have already exceeded that stage."

The somewhat brief and less than rewarding meeting was brought to a close but with everyone expressing a determination to **find that plot.**

Worryingly, two weeks went by without any success in the pursuit of a burial site. There had been a couple of offers from those with plots of land big enough but, alas, none was in a location that could in any way represent the special significance that such a hallowed site would need. Meanwhile the Minister of Bethel Chapel was getting a little anxious over the time the miners remains were occupying the Chapel Hall; though he emphasized that he was 'just concerned but not complaining'-which was a little ambiguous.

Then out of the blue, Max Forester had a phone call from Reverend Thorn, vicar of the parish church who, for personal as well as communal reasons, was profoundly interested in locating and appropriating a burial site for the miners.

"Hello Mr Forester, I understand you have not had any success in locating a suitable site for the Pentrebach Level miners' interment. I am full of praise Mr Forester for the time and dedicated effort you and those assisting you in this endeavour have already given and for which reason you must be a very busy man. However, I will be grateful if you could find the time to call at the church sometime today, as I have something to suggest that might lead to a possible solution to your problem."

"Believe me vicar; I am available for such a visit whenever you have the time to meet me. If you are at the church now I will be more than happy to pop round this instant."

"I am at the vicarage at the moment, Mr Forester, but if we both make our way to the church we should arrive at much the same time."

"Thank you very much vicar, I am on my way."

It didn't take Forester long to get to the church and after a few minutes wait, along came the vicar. Forester was anxious to learn what it was the vicar was going to say; especially as he had hinted at a possible solution to the burial site problem. At the same time, however, he couldn't imagine what it was; clearly it had nothing to do with the church graveyard; with no available space there.

After the familiar greetings, the vicar opened the church gates and Forester followed him in.

"If you'll follow me Mr Forester, we'll walk through the graveyard to the furthest wall."

When they had reached the wall the vicar pointed to a stone plinth up against the wall with room for both of them to stand on.

"What do you see on the other side Mr Forester?" the vicar asked.

"Well nothing, just weeds and bramble vicar."

"That's right, and see how far it extends before it reaches the fence of that field. Now to the right it reaches out to the old manor road, which goes on beyond the church to the ruins of Afan Manor House. To the left it extends to Nant–gan-yr-Eithin, stream of the gorse; just a little brook that runs by. As you can see, Mr Forester, it covers a considerable area. And as far as I know, after some thirty years as vicar, it has never been used for anything; just left to overgrow."

Of course Forester could see what the vicar was hinting at but the overriding question immediately sprung to his mind.

"Whose land is it vicar?"

"Well Mr Forester, I can only think of one possible owner and that would be the current descendent of the Watkins Afan Manor House family."

"And do you know who that is vicar?"

"Alas, I do not. I know that the family abandoned the House in 1912 when Rees Watkins died with a sudden heart-attack. Apparently, his wife had predeceased him having contracted consumption, TB as we know it today. There was no male heir and the two daughters married into wealthy families, joining their husbands to settle elsewhere. I understand that one settled somewhere in Kent and the other near Gloucester. But they will, if still alive, be in their seventies by now. What I do know is that there are some people in the village still paying rent to the Watkins' Estate, I believe through a local solicitor."

"Vicar, you have given me so much fresh hope, I am truly grateful. I will make enquiries to see if I can contact the Estate Management, probably the solicitor you just referred to, and find out if that piece of land can be acquired. It's absolutely the best place we could have hoped for; right on top of the church and with easy access. This is a wonderful opportunity vicar, I cannot thank you enough."

Immediately upon his return home Forester phoned Ben Collins and told him what he had learned from the vicar.

"Max this is wonderful news, don't worry about making enquiries, I know the solicitor who deals with the Estate business. I am aware that a few houses that are not on the council list or locally privately owned do still belong to the Watkins' family. I'll get on to him right away and let you know what he says; this is great news Max, great news. By the way, the NCB have agreed to make a contribution; either physically –help in developing a burial site- or monetarily, if we are short of money. I think this is a benevolent gesture and I have already taken it upon myself to thank them. I hope that's alright with you Max?"

"Absolutely Ben, suddenly things are going in the right direction, let us hope it continues that way."

Within a few hours Ben Collins was back in touch with Forester, having spoken to the Afan Estate solicitor, he learned that Mrs Elizabeth Stanford nee Watkins, who was now seventy five, was the sole surviving daughter of Rees Watkins the last Squire of Afan Manor House Estate, her sister Mary, one year older, having recently passed on. They were granddaughters of William Watkins, who was in possession of the Estate during the time of the Pentrebach Level.

"Both sisters have children, Max, Elizabeth has one son and Mary two daughters. It is Elizabeth's son, Edward, who handles any business connected with the Pentrebach family Estate.

"The solicitor, Mr Andrew Cosby, got in touch with Edward Stanford while I was there Max, and he has agreed to pay us a visit, calling at the Council Offices, next week. Apparently, he had heard of the recovery of the lost miners and had intended contacting the NCB to learn what it entailed and whether his family might be of some assistance. This is incredible Max, I feel sure that he will, at the very least, negotiate a deal over that land. I explained where the land we are interested in is and he promised to bring something along to determine whether it belonged to his family or not. He is to arrive at here at 2 pm on Wednesday next, so be here Max and bring along anyone you think should be present."

"As you say Ben, this is wonderful news; yes, of course I'll be there and I'm sure Frank will want to be there too. I look forward to it with great optimism Ben; we now have the people, the Council, the NCB, the NUM and the Watkins family showing an active interest in this project, I truly believe there has never been nor will there ever be, a collective effort like this one."

Max Forester and Frank Lewis had arrived at Ben Collins' office on the following Wednesday afternoon about half an hour early and they were seated chatting with Ben Collins and his colleague Bryn Thomas, when a young office girl knocked and opened the door, to announce the arrival of Mr Edward Stanford who was accompanied by his son.

Edward Stanford was in his early fifties and his son, Robert was twenty-five. Edward's mother, Elizabeth, was the last in the Watkins family line; with her marriage and that of her older deceased sister Mary, the name of Watkins was lost.

The father was a tall lean man with a head of mostly brown but greying hair. He was a good looking man sporting a thin moustache and dark brown eyes. He spoke, as would be expected, with an educated tongue, articulate and clear. He introduced his son explaining that Robert had taken an interest in the Pentrebach Level disaster, after having heard it referred to many times by his grandmother –in fact it was an event much talked of by the family over the years- and had expressed a wish to come along and meet people for whom the disaster had so much personal meaning.

"You are both very welcome Mr Stanford," Ben Collins declared, "This is my colleague Mr Bryn Thomas and here Mr Max Forester and Mr Frank Lewis, Chairman and Secretary of the local NUM Lodge respectively. I don't know how much you already know about our quest to bring about a final appropriate resting place for the recently recovered miners of the Pentrebach Level disaster of 1863. I will point out that it was Mr Forester who initiated the move to ensure that the miners' remains were retained in the village and not, as was the earlier intention, removed and disposed of by the government. We are all indebted to him for his foresight and actions"

Forester responded by assuring the two gentlemen that the progress since his early intervention, was as a result of a people's valley-wide effort, with Mr Collins himself playing a pivotal role.

It was Forester who explained the reason for contacting the Watkins, or rather the Stanford, family. He told the two gentlemen that the project had one more hurdle to overcome; that of acquiring a suitable site for the burial of those twenty-five men and boys. He then went on to relate his meeting with the parish vicar and their discussion over the land contiguous to the church graveyard; it now rested upon whose land it is and obtaining their consent to negotiate its use as a burial site.

Edward Stanford expressed his admiration for the incredible resolve of all those concerned in this project:

"That the sacrifice those miners made can finally be given a deserved place of permanent recognition; is truly remarkable.

"While they remained lost to the outside world," Mr Stanford added, "I can appreciate that memorial plaques and worthy notices were all that you could ascribe to them. Now, with their recovery, the opportunity for a dedicated, hallowed spot, which future generations can visit and pay their respects has arisen, I can see why you are so enthusiastic gentlemen.

"I have brought along a map of the old Afan Manor Estate which illustrates that which is still in the hands of our family. We currently own just four houses as most of the Estate property and land has been sold to farmers and developers. However, there are a few pockets of land that have not been taken up for one reason or another. You say that the plot you are interested in lies contiguous to the parish church, so let us look to the map and determine whether we still own it or not and we can go from there."

The map was rolled out over the table around which they were all seated and pinned down at four corners with paper weights; all eyes eagerly began to scrutinise the document in search of that now much regarded spot.

"That's it there," Forester indicated to Mr Stanford.

"Well, Mr Forester, you're in luck, those areas lightly shaded in blue are still in our hands and as you can see, although there are not many, that location is coloured thus. Before we take up the business of legitimate transfer however, which I will get my solicitor to carry out, I'd be grateful if Robert and I could pay a visit to the site today while we are here?"

It was Ben Collins who replied to this request.

"Of course," Mr Stanford, "I'm sure we will all be delighted to accompany you; what do you say gentlemen?"

It was soon arranged that the two councillors and NUM officials would travel in one car and the Stanfords follow on behind. Forester had phoned the vicar who agreed to be at the church upon their arrival.

The journey took about twenty minutes and the vicar was, as arranged, waiting at the church gate to greet the party. He was keen to meet the two Stanfords as many of their ancestors lay entombed in the church vaults and there were a number of memorial plaques dedicated to their memories displayed about the walls of the church interior.

But first he led them to the outer graveyard wall to inspect the land under review.

Mr Stanford expressed his agreement that the plot was ideal for the purpose and his delight that it was also available.

"Gentlemen," he declared, "I am as pleased with this as you are. The Pentrebach Level disaster has not only cast a shadow over this village and surrounding area for all these years, but has weighed heavily on the Watkins/Stanford family too. We, none of us, can be held accountable for the actions or inactions of our ancestors but sometimes we inherit them nonetheless. It is widely viewed that the failure to introduce a Return Airway into the Penrebach mine, led to the miners not having an alternative exit route which might have saved their lives.

I have studied the mining practices of the time and the laws pertaining to the mine owners' and landowners' legal obligations and learned that their inaction at Pentrebach was not in breach of any law and this was confirmed at the official Hearing that followed the disaster; though the presiding judge did make and aside to a possible opportunity missed by the mine owners. He pointed out that other mine owners in the district had cut or driven airways early in their mine's history and that one day this practice may become obligatory. He wasn't to know it but as early as 1865, just two years on, an Act of Parliament made it obligatory to have two shafts or outlets for all mines.

William Watkins, my maternal great grandfather, was but the landowner and therefore not responsible for the running of the mine. Nonetheless, we his descendants yet feel that as a substantial beneficiary he might have been able to apply some pressure to bear on the mine management to bring about this much needed airway; and it is this which has left us with an uncomfortable family legacy with regard to the disaster."

This sudden and unexpected revelation by Mr Stanford took the others completely by surprise and for a moment no one said anything. It was the vicar who broke the silence.

"Mr Stanford, that is a very sincere and brave statement to make but I don't believe you or your family have anything to reproach yourselves for. As you so rightly say, the apparent errors or inactions of ones forefathers cannot be brought to bear upon oneself, or other contemporary relatives. One of the men lost in the Pentrebach Level disaster was Samuel Thorn, my grandfather's brother and as a result of a surviving document; a notebook kept by one of the Deputies, we have been granted an authentic day to day account of what took place in that mine.

"Samuel Thorn was the mine's Repairer, just twenty-four years old at the time, who was responsible for the general maintenance of the mine's Main thoroughfare. This involved the care of the dramroad when road spikes or rails came lose. On the day of the explosion he attended to a gap in the rails by levering the two parted rails together when, a more adequate job was required. He should have sought help and with two men working, they could have raised the rails and realigned and secured them.

As the result of a complaint by the men over the quality of air, they had been delayed by their efforts to persuade the Overman to take their grievance to the management. Sam Thorn had decided to attend to the gap as he did because he did not want to be the cause of any further delay in the men getting the coal out. Tending to the gap in the rails as he did was not an uncommon practice as very often he was unable to get assistance anyway. However, when the first journey of drams was being hauled out of the mine the weight of the drams re-opened the gap in the rails and sparks from the friction ignited some unknown pockets of gas, which caused the explosion.

"Sam Thorn came under fire from the Deputy –writer of the notes- for his actions but later realising that he only acted as he did out of concern for the men, the Deputy apologised, assuring him that he could not have foreseen events and was in no way to blame. And I, as Sam Thorn's descendant relative, do not harbour any discomfort as a result of his actions."

"Gentlemen, gentlemen, please," Forester interjected, "the Pentrebach Level accident, and that is what it was, took place over ninety years ago. These were entirely different times and while there is much the Victorians did that we would not sanction or approve of today, we cannot and should not judge their practices retrospectively. The vicar is quite right Mr Stanford, when he says he does not harbour any discomfort over a decision made by his ancestor and nor should you. The tragedy of 1863 at Pentrebach was unfortunate but it was 1863, and that is where it belongs."

Everyone seemed calmed by Forester's remarks and later, Forester and Ben Collins, referring to the incident, concluded that both Edward Stanford and the vicar appeared anxious to get their respective issues out in the open, rather, as they may have thought, than either being brought up later by a third party. That neither case was looked upon with any condemnation must have pleased both men and they must also have felt assured that they will hear nothing more of them.

Before leaving the vicar took them on a tour of the church, primarily for the benefit of the Stanfords, though the other four accompanied them. He pointed out various memorial tributes to the earlier Watkins family members and told Edward that one of them, a certain George Watkins, long before the Pentrebach mine days, had contributed a large sum of money to renovate the church which was in serious need of repair at the time.

During this tour Forester and the two councillors approached the vicar with regard to his conducting the funeral service when the burials take place; to which he remarked that he would have been disappointed' if he had not been asked, so that was settled. Back at the Council Office Mr Stanford made it clear that he intended to donate the land to the cause and was prepared to let the NUM or the Council or any appropriate authority they might suggest, become the official new land owners.

Both Forester and Ben Collins were delighted with this outcome, expressing their sincere gratitude to Mr Stanford for his generosity. It was agreed that the land should pass to the perpetual possession of Pentrebach Village, a decision Mr Stanford was more than pleased with. Before leaving Mr Stanford phoned his local solicitor, Mr Andrew Cosby, and asked him to expect a visit from one or other of those representing the Pentrebach Miners' burial cause, with an appropriate letter of authorisation granting a portion of land agreed by him to be transferred to their ownership.

He also requested that he be allowed to return and discuss anything he might be able to help with, in creating the burial site. Both Forester and Collins expressed their willingness that he should get involved to whatever degree he desired.

20

Forester had held a meeting of the village committee to inform them of the progress made. Earlier, he had called on Bernard Carter the Minister of Bethel Chapel, to bring him the same news. However, he was reluctantly obliged to tell the Minister that there was much to do before any burials could take place. Thankfully, the Minister, in what appeared to be a change of heart from his earlier response, assured Forester that there was no need to hurry as they would not require the use of the hall until later in the year. This was very good news to Forester. Everyone at the meeting was delighted with the response from the Stanford family and pleased that they had shown such care and compassion.

Forester had decided that it was better they heard, from him, of Edward Stanford's regret, over the failure by William Watkins to put pressure on the mine owners to initiate the Return Airway or Shaft at the old mine and how his family had carried 'an uncomfortable legacy' as a result. He added that it had been established that there had been no breach of the law over this issue on the part of the owners of the mine but that a moral obligation might have been expected. He once again stressed that they were different times with different values and we should leave the Victorian ways in the Victorian age. There was not one voice of dissension from the audience.

A few days later Forester and Collins were back at the site calculating how much land there was available and the task of removing the bramble and weeds, so that access to the site and the layout of the graves could be planned. Judging by eye alone, being unable to carry out any meaningful measurements, the two men were satisfied that the area will easily cater for the twenty-five graves; as far as they were concerned a communal grave was not even up for discussion.

The work of removing the bramble and weeds from the burial site was soon undertaken by the NCB –free of charge- and with the ground now visible and clear; plans were being discussed as to the actual layout the burial site should take.

So far everything had been achieved without cost: removal and storage of the miners' remains, obtaining the burial site and having it cleared of all weed and debris. But Forester and the others were well aware that there would be quite some money needed to pay for the eventual site perimeter wall; cost of the burials and graves and any other embellishments they may wish to add.

The ladies of the WI had raised a large sum from their jumble sales, arts and crafts sales and much more from their well-practiced fund raising efforts. They had also spread the word among the WI branches throughout the neighbouring valleys, which had been met with very favourable response. Collection boxes had been placed in pubs and shops and there had been a number of independent donations, not least that from the NCB and the NUM. So, all in all, there was a healthy financial pot available.

It was time to begin the task of organising the burial site and arranging the funerals. A temporary wire fence was raised around the burial ground, leaving a wide gap where the road passed by, which was to be kept clear as an access point. After engaging a surveyor, a plan was drawn up, which illustrated ten graves along the field-side, each grave lying length ways from the field towards the church, A further ten graves parallel with the opposite ten along the church grave-yard wall, lying length ways from the wall to the path, with a wide path running down the centre. At the lower end, above the stream, five graves lying length ways across the site with an open clear space between them and the stream.

A copy of this plan was on display at the Pentrebach library, the NUM office and the Council Offices at Aber-

Afon-Gwen. Out of courtesy one was also sent to Edward Stanford who, after receiving it, phoned Forester and asked if he might be permitted to suggest a change to the plan.

"As it is, Mr Forester, I notice that there will be no access from the village church to the burial site," Stanford, pointed out. "Could I therefore suggest that a part of the graveyard wall be removed and a lich gate inserted, which I am prepared to pay for. I realise that the graves nearest the graveyard wall on the plan will have to be spaced differently to cater for a path to join the principle path but judging from the dimensions shown, I believe this could be achieved without much trouble; I also noticed during my visit, that there is already a path through the graveyard, which we walked along to get a view of over the wall."

"To begin with Mr Stanford I will be happy if you will in future address me as Max, as most people do. I think your suggestion is an excellent idea and it is very generous of to offer to meet the cost. A lich gate would undoubtedly enhance the appearance of the site and will be most in keeping with the character of the church. I will, of course, have to consult with the others and the vicar, who I'm sure, will have to seek permission from the church authorities; I will set about making the necessary enquiries immediately and get back to you with the outcome. I do not anticipate any objections, far from it I am confident it will be met with pleasure and gratitude."

"Thank you Max and I agree with dropping the formalities, so it will be Edward from now on. I look forward to your call and hope that your optimism is upheld."

When Forester told Ben Collins of Stanford's offer he was delighted and the same response was forthcoming from all the committee members. The vicar too was very keen on the idea and promised to get in touch with the church authorities immediately to seek their permission.

It wasn't long before the vicar invited Forester to the vicarage telling him that he had had the response over the lich gate from the church authorities, which he wished to discuss with him over a cup of tea.

"They are more than happy to agree to the lich gate, Mr Forester but there is something else they would like to see done. They want to invite the Bishop to come to the site before any work has commenced and hold a ceremony of consecration; that the burial ground will receive the official blessing of the church. They appreciate that the land does not belong to the church but as the funeral service will be conducted in the customary Christian manner, you having already asked me to officiate, and as the ground lies contiguous to the parish church, consecrating the ground does seem to be in keeping with custom and protocol.

"I will raise the matter with the committee vicar, though I can hardly imagine anyone objecting. I am sure everyone will want this burial site to become the hallowed land that it will undoubtedly represent. You will recall how the site of the Pentrebach Level and surrounds were treated with similar reverence."

Forester got in touch with Mr Stanford and explained the church authorities' response to the lich gate, adding the appeal for the Bishop to consecrate the burial site. Mr Stanford was delighted and agreed with Forester that there was unlikely to be any objection. He also told Forester that he would very much like to attend the miners' interment ceremony along with his son Robert. Forester responded by assuring him that he will inform him well in advance of the date set for the funerals, when of course he and his son will be more than welcome.

As predicted by Forester there was total agreement in favour of the Bishop's visit. It, in fact, turned out to be a much attended day with crowds filling the road and, with permission from the farmer, the adjacent field. The council officials and representatives of the NCB and, of course Forester and Frank Lewis on behalf of the NUM were also present.

A further committee meeting was held to debate arrangements for the grave digging and the actual funerals. It was decided to approach a local construction company to dig and prepare the twenty-five graves but there was some difficulty in reaching agreement on the way in which the coffins would be conveyed to the site. The idea of hiring twenty-five hearses was not only impractical but nigh on impossible. Throughout the valley there were three funeral directors, all of whom had just the one hearse. Two of them had standby horse-drawn carriage hearses but it was felt that they would look out of place in such a procession. Taking this into consideration it was calculated that in order to get hold of twenty-five hearses, they would need to call upon undertakers from far and wide. It was Ben Collins who came up with a more practical solution.

"Let us assume that we can get hold of five hearses. The distance from the Bethel Chapel Hall to the burial site is only a little over two miles, so why don't we make five journeys carrying five coffins each time? Yes, it will take some time but this a going to be a very noteworthy occasion and consequently, should be conducted in an orderly and controlled manner. No one will be in a hurry to get through the ceremony, which will mean that everyone, young and old will experience a day of such significance that it will long remain in their memories and be an event that they will refer to and talk about for many years to come; one that will be passed down from generation to generation, as indeed we would all wish it to be."

This solution, providing five hearses could be obtained, which appeared much more likely than twenty-five, was unanimously supported. After much further debate Forester read out the finally agreed plan.

"Each of the first five coffins arriving at the burial site will be carried from the hearses on the shoulders of four bearers —aware that the coffins would not be heavy- and placed on planks close to the furthest five graves, those running alongside the stream. Then a batch of five coffins along the field side row, then the church side row and the same repeated with the remaining ten coffins.

"The bearers in turn will remain at the grave sides and before the ceremonial activities are commenced, in response to an arranged signal, they will take up the straps placed beneath the coffins and simultaneously lower the twenty five coffins into the graves. This will entail a hundred men working in perfect unison to bring the burials to a close. At this point the vicar will begin to conduct the service during which, others, myself included, who have agreed to speak, will do so and there will also be two hymns sung by the Pentrebach Male Voice Choir. "

Before the meeting closed a twelve year old boy –the same age as the youngest boy lost in the disaster- was called to draw two tickets out of ten which had been placed in a hat containing the titles of ten different hymns.

"The two selected hymns to be sung by the choir will be: Abide with Me and Amazing Grace." Forester announced.

Everyone was well pleased with the details and the meeting ended on a positive note.

The local construction company was prepared to dig and prepare the graves under the guidance of the appointed surveyor and this went ahead smoothly. The three valley funeral directors were only too pleased to be part of this unique funeral procession and it was they who contacted a further two funeral directors from other districts; in order that the five hearses required were made available.

All was now ready. The burial site with its temporary wire fence and open graves was left exposed with the access gap at the church roadside. The only decision to be taken now was the date of the funeral. After consultation with the five funeral directors and organising the hundred volunteer bearers; arrangements agreed with the vicar and the Pentrebach Male Voice Choir; the agreed date was Tuesday May 30th 1957.

Notices to that effect were posted throughout the valley and appeared in the obituary columns of the two local newspapers and of course, on the Church and Chapel notice boards. Forester decided to write to Edward Stanford rather than phone, that he would have a detailed summary of the proposed day's proceedings.

"Dear Edward,

I am writing to you –having obtained your address from Mr Andrew Cosby- rather than phoning, to inform you of the details of the Pentrebach Level miners' burial arrangements and date. This unique funeral will take place on Tuesday 30th May and I sincerely hope that you and your son Robert can attend as you indicated your desire so to do. I am delighted to say that, after some complicated arrangements we have been able to arrive at what we believe is the best outcome, which will enable us to convey and bury the twenty-five men and boys in a single location of twenty-five graves.

Of course you are already familiar with the site, which is now prepared with the twenty-five graves dug and the intersecting paths laid out. A temporary wire fence has been raised around the site leaving an opening on the manor road side as a means of entry. The coffins will be conveyed to the burial site in batches of five as it was agreed that this number was the most practical. Apart from its impracticality, we were never going to find twenty-five hearses as was first proposed. The first batch will depart from Bethel Chapel Hall at 10.00 am. The journey is approximately four miles to the burial site and back. This will, therefore, be repeated five times.

When the burials have taken place and the earth allowed time to settle, we will set about laying appropriate grave stones and a monolith will be raised with suitable memorial details and the names of all the men and boys inscribed thereon.

Later, it is intended to raise a stone wall around the site with two access points; a gate in the location of the opening onto the manor roadside and your very generously gifted lich gate.

Please do not feel that this is in anyway an obligation but if you would like to speak at the funeral, let me know and I will include your name on the service programme.

I look forward to your presence on the day with great pleasure.

Yours sincerely,

Max

Edward also replied in writing:

Dear Max,

You and your voluntary group of helpers are to be applauded for the wonderful job you have carried out, in achieving your determined aim to arrange and secure a final dignified resting place of special significance, for the twenty-five men and boys who were and would have remained forever lost; effecting an enduring conscious burden upon all those influenced by their tragic circumstances.

Robert and I will most certainly attend the miners' burials and what I'm sure will be a funeral ceremony of noteworthy significance. I firmly believe that the site of the Pentrebach Miners' graves will become a much visited place of homage. I will deem it an honour and privilege to be allowed to speak during the service and thank you for making this possible.

Until Tuesday May 30th,

I am yours sincerely,

Edward

21

The Funeral

Tuesday 30th May 1957 turned out to be a calm and sunny day. As if in response to the weather the valley also seemed particularly calm; this was encouraged by the fact that all the shops and businesses were closed for the day, a decision taken by the Aber-Afon-Gwen town council and agreed by those concerned.

There was, however, some activity in and around the village of Pentrebach as early as eight o'clock that morning. The police were engaged in closing all roads abutting those along the two mile route the five funeral hearses will travel on, from Bethel Chapel Hall to the prepared burial site, five times.

By nine o'clock the village was filling with traffic, as vehicles belonging to those from throughout the valley and beyond, began to occupy every available space. Vicar Thorn had arrived at the church and joined a small gathering of NCB officials with Frank Lewis, NUM and Bryn Thomas of Aber-Afon-Gwen Council. A stage platform had been raised just inside the field close to the perimeter fence, which those who will be involved in the presentation of the service will occupy and it was here that the group were talking amongst themselves.

Back at Bethel Chapel Hall were Max Forester and Ben Collins. They had decided to stay there to help organise the coffins safely onto the hearses and on their way. They would follow together in a car behind the last five hearses. Edward Stanford and his son Robert would accompany them. Each batch of five hearses would be accompanied by five cars, which would be used on each successive journey, to carry twenty volunteer bearers who, upon their arrival at the burial site would take their place in groups of four to carry the coffins to the respective graves, where they would wait until all twenty five coffins had arrived. All in all it had to be a well organised and perfectly timed operation with all those with a part to play adhering to a well-practiced plan.

Soon the area around and about the burial site was becoming ever more congested as crowds converged. All along the funeral route people amassed to witness this unique succession of hearses as the first five left Bethel Chapel Hall. Many would stay to watch all the repeated journeys.

The field beyond the burial site fence was a throng of people. In order to ensure the safe passage of the bearers to the graves and provide room for the choir, only those involved were allowed into the burial site area. Loud speakers had been set up on numerous nearby trees and lampposts to enable the service to be heard far and wide.

With the arrival of the final five hearses and the last five cars of bearers followed by the car containing Max Forester, Ben Collins and Edward and Robert Stanford, it appeared that everyone from the valley and even beyond had made their way to attend this very special funeral congregation.

Those taking part in the ceremony had made their way to their respective positions. On the temporary raised stage platform a row of chairs were occupied by the reverend Thorn and the three volunteer speakers: Max Forester, Edward Stanford and Collin Wright. Standing alongside each grave were four bearers; and also standing –behind the five graves at the far end of the site- the Pentrebach Male Voice Choir.

The service was to start at exactly eleven o'clock but two minutes before eleven the vicar rose to face the several microphones at the head of the stage. In respect for his position and in anticipation of the ceremony commencing, the crowd responded with complete silence. For the next couple of minutes nothing stirred; the birds could be clearly heard in the neighbouring trees and even the gentle flow of Nant-gan-yr-Eithin murmuring by.

At precisely eleven O'clock the church bell rang out and simultaneously, by previous arrangement, the colliery hooter sounded loud and clear, across the valley. Those on the stage rose and bowed their heads and the entire congregation reciprocated instinctively. Both the bell and the hooter continued for one whole minute, after which the vicar thanked everyone for their display of common deference.

"Friends, neighbours and fellow citizens," he continued, "I have officiated over many funerals in this parish over the past thirty years but today we are here to witness a funeral like no other. It is customary to use a funeral to celebrate the life of the deceased. In this instance, under these far from normal circumstances, we are unable to do this; not only because this is a funeral of so many but because we, none of us, are familiar with any of the lives of the deceased. So today we will instead, celebrate the recovery and return of the twenty-five men and boys brought back to us by a revelation of chance.

I, as a Christian, believe that the hand of God may also have had something to do with it. And today all Christians here present, will share my belief that those twenty-five poor souls lost for ninety-three years, are now at last passing into God's safe keeping."

As he spoke he raised his hand high in the air and the one hundred bearers took the strain of the coffins' straps and gently and simultaneously lowered each one into their respective graves.

"In the name of the Father the Son and the Holy Ghost we commend these twenty-five souls to the earth, in the sure and certain hope of everlasting life. 'There are many rooms in my mansion' sayeth the Lord, may these twenty-five souls find space in God's heaven and the rest, peace and tranquillity it assures."

The vicar then announced that, "The Male Voice Choir will now sing the hymn 'Abide with Me.'

After the hymn the vicar sat down and Collin Wright, colliery manager, approached the microphones.

"Ladies and Gentlemen, I very much doubt that those of us present here today will ever see the like of it in our lifetimes again. For over ninety years the victims of the Pentrebach Level disaster remained lost and the village had become synonymous with their entrapment. While it was one among many mining tragedies, it was unique in that not only were all its victims' lives lost, their bodies were never recovered.

"Until today not one was to have the dignity of a Christian burial; leaving relatives to grieve without their presence. It's difficult to imagine how those relatives could have found any succour or comfort in the total absence of their departed loved ones. There are people yet living in the village today, who have descended from or are related to, one or other of the Pentrebach Level victims. For them this must be a poignant moment but they can take some degree of solace from having lived to see this day of their relatives' return. For us all, it is a time to honour the victims and be thankful that it has fallen to us in our time, to grant them the dignity of a public and Christian burial. May they all rest in peace."

The manager returned to his seat and Edward Stanford moved to the front of the stage.

"Ladies and Gentlemen, It will be quite understandable if most of you do not recognise me or understand why a stranger is addressing you on a day when the event is all about local people and your village and valley. My name is Edward Stanford and William Watkins, owner of the Afon Manor Estate, was my maternal great grandfather. So this day is also important to me, in that my family have, down the years, shared your burden of loss over the tragic accident at Pentrebach Level. Regrettably, I cannot change the circumstances surrounding the events leading up to the tragedy but must, as we all must, remember that ninety-three years ago life and its ways, rules and effects were entirely different. I ask that we, therefore, come together today and share in our relief and gratitude at being given the opportunity to witness the blessing of the Christian burials of our recovered Pentrebach heroes. I thank you for your attention and understanding."

Edward Stanford resumed his seat amid a courteous silence.

Finally, Max Forester moved to the front of the stage and, in what must have been an unprecedented response for a funeral, was received with a mass applause which lasted for a full minute. As the applause subsided he was seen to be emotionally moved by this spontaneous and overwhelmingly genuine acknowledgement.

"Ladies and Gentlemen," he began, uncharacteristically inhibited, "you give me far more credit than I deserve. Arriving at where we are today; bringing these lost miners from relative obscurity to public awareness could never have been achieved by one man. So, with your permission I would like to extend your generous applause to all the others; without whom this wonderful day would not have been possible.

"Let us not forget that but for a chance geological event of some fifty million years ago which, in disturbing the strata, diverted the direction of our coalface, we would not have stumbled upon the old Pentrebach Level and the lost miners. The vicar might well be right when he said God may have had a hand in it.

"Whatever the cause and subsequent developments, we are here and so are the lost miners' of Pentrebach Level and I and everyone here today, rejoices in this moment. We are grateful for this splendid burial site to Mr Edward Stanford and his family who gave us the land. When the site is complete, we estimate in a few weeks' time, there will be a stone wall surrounding it with two access points. One will be that which we used today, with an improved entrance and the other a lich gate from the church graveyard, which will undoubtedly enhance the site's appearance. And for this too we will be indebted to Mr Stanford.

"We are also indebted to the NCB for clearing and preparing the site and making a substantial donation to our fund. The NUM too has made a generous contribution and has worked alongside me in helping with the necessary arrangements. The Aber-Afon-Gwen town council through the good offices of Councillor Ben Collins and colleagues, helped to overcome what would have been a number of official impediments. Councillor Collins was always there whenever I needed his help. To the Minister of Bethel Chapel and the chapel members and Deacons, for their kind permission to store the miners' remains in their Chapel Hall we are also most indebted. And it would certainly be remiss of me to overlook the tireless efforts of the Ladies of the Women's Institute, who staged all manner of events to raise a most substantial sum for our cause. Finally, I cannot over emphasize the contribution of the village committee set up for the sole purpose of making this day a reality.

"I would now like to hand you back to the gentleman who it was pointed out this site to me in the first place, even though neither he nor I had any idea at the time, who owned it: the Reverend Desmond Thorn, Vicar of this Parish."

"Thank you Mr Forester and thank you one and all, for attending here today to pay your respects and give thanks to God for the gift of the return of the miners of Pentrebach Level. The Village Male Voice Choir will now bring the service to a close by inviting you all to join them in singing the very well-known, "Amazing Grace" so appropriate for the occasion: Thus the ceremony was brought to a close.

As the crowd began to disperse Edward Stanford approached Max Forester and asked him if, when the burial site is complete, he might be invited to come and see it.

"But of course Edward, the builders will be starting the wall next week, it is to be a double-lined stone wall which will have the appearance of antiquity, as the builders are a specialist firm. Fortunately, we have sufficient funds to pay for this and the full length flat grave stones which will cover each grave. There is also to be a monolith inscribed with the appropriate memorial details and the miners' names and, of course, your lich-gate. It should take about six or seven weeks to complete the site and I must admit I am looking forward to seeing the finished work myself. Any monies left over will be placed in a special account and used towards the care and maintenance of the site in the future. When the work is complete we will hold an 'open-day' so that the community can visit the site as an expression of deference; I will let you know Edward when we have agreed upon a date."

Before Stanford left Forester referred to the Clive Harding note book; which the vicar had raised on his first visit. He found it incredibly interesting and asked if he might be allowed to view it when he returns. Forester assured him that he would consult with the NCB and try to arrange a viewing.

It didn't take long for the crowd to leave and a local company move in with two small mechanical shovels to set about filling the graves. The lost miners of Pentrebach Level had finally found their last resting place.

22

Within six weeks the stone wall including the two access points had been established. Each of the twenty-five graves had been covered with a full length horizontal stone three bricks high, the centres of which engraved with a crossed shovel and mandrel. A five foot monolith stood at the centre of the site against the wall running parallel with the field; At its head was engraved a pony (cob) attached to a dram of coal; a symbol of respect for the four cobs lost in the disaster. It had been decided to leave their remains in the mine. Beneath the engraving was inscribed an appropriate epitaph accompanied by the names of the twenty-five victims.

The date of the 'open-day' turned out to be Sunday 6th of August. On the preceding Monday Forester had phoned Stanford to let him know.

"That's wonderful news Max. I will of course be there and, if it's agreeable with you, Robert and my wife and mother would also like to attend."

"But of course Edward, we will be delighted to meet them. The time of the meeting will be 2.0 pm and we will congregate in the field behind the site, by kind permission of the farmer, where vicar Thorn will address the crowd. After the service the people can visit the site in procession via the entrance from the old manor road and progress through the site leaving through the lich-gate and the graveyard.

"If you and your family can make your way to the Miners' Welfare Hall an hour or so before hand, Edward, Ben Collins and I will be there and we will arrange some refreshments for you before we journey to the site."

"That is very kind of you Max; I look forward to this most interesting and significant day with great pleasure."

The Welfare Hall was a buzz of low voices when the Stanfords arrived. Forester and Ben Collins had placed themselves near the foyer in anticipation of their arrival and soon they were being introduced to the extended Stanford family.

Mrs Elizabeth Stanford, now in her seventies, proved to be an interesting woman who could recall her childhood at the Afon Manor House as being a happy time in her life.

"My father, Rees Watkins, died in 1912 and with him our family name. Mary my elder sister had already married and left home, I was married and my husband and I had lived part time in the manor until my father passed on. At that time I was thirty years old and the house was simply beyond our ability to maintain. Besides which Seymour, my husband, an architect, needed to live where his work took him and so we had no alternative but to leave. Despite our best endeavours my sister and I found no one interested in taking such an extensive property on and, as you undoubtedly know, the house fell into disrepair and finally into dereliction. Such was the fate of many country houses in the early twentieth century as lifestyles changed so quickly. But I'm sure you don't want to hear me babbling on about my past gentlemen?"

"On the contrary, Mrs Stanford," responded Ben Collins, "yours is an interesting story."

Edward Stanford's wife, Julia, was a pleasant woman who was keen to congratulate all those concerned with the task of recovering the miners and all the effort that must have gone into arriving at this stage.

"Edward has kept me up to date with the sequence of events and I have nothing but admiration for you all." She exclaimed.

Robert Stanford had a special request to put to Forester. He wanted to know if it could be arranged at some time in the future, for him to visit the new Pentrebach Level as he had always wanted to see what a working colliery looked like. Forester promised him that he would seek permission from the NCB but added that he did not envisage any problem and would get in touch with him as soon as he could arrange such a visit.

They all had time to sample the excellent buffet table, laid on by the faithful women of the W. I. before leaving for the burial site.

Upon arrival Max Forester, Ben Collins and the Stanfords joined the ever growing crowd as they made their way into the field contiguous to the burial site. Once again a platform stage, though smaller, had been erected to cater this time for Reverend Desmond Thorn only –as agreed by all concerned- who would address the audience. It was felt that it would be inappropriate on this occasion for there to be a further run of speeches, which might appear repetitive.

When the vicar ascended the stage silence alighted upon the crowd as a mist descending upon a mountaintop.

"We have assembled here today to pay homage and respect to the Pentrebach Level miners now buried in the consecrated site behind us. And what a magnificent site it is. In the days past when I have walked through it, I am filled with regard for the people who worked so hard to make this place a reality; for the love and devotion which inspired their actions; for the craftsmen who made it physically possible and for the communal endeavour that brought it about.

"Nothing will ever erase the tragedy of that day in January 1863 when twenty-one men and four young lads were lost; seemingly for ever. But today we can celebrate, yes, celebrate their recovery. For everyone here and everyone who will visit this burial site from now on will recognise that they did come home in the end. Let us, therefore, give thanks to God for their return and I ask you now to join with me in the Lord's Prayer."

After the Lord's Prayer, the vicar invited the people to make their way slowly, in procession, via the Manor House road gate, through the burial site and on through, what he described as the magnificent lich-gate, and then to proceed passed the church. He asked if they would be kind enough to keep moving but at the same time enjoy and appreciate the site.

This they seem to do, as it took quite some time before the last of the visitors filed out of the graveyard. But not everyone had left. Max Forester, Ben Collins and the Stanfords remained in the field along with vicar Thorn, Collin Wright and Doctor Carmichael, who had made the trip from London at Forester's invitation. Before they set of for the burial site Forester approached Edward Stanford and handed him a something.

"You will recall my telling you about the Clive Harding note book, Edward, found at the scene of the location of the lost miners?" He announced. "Well in cooperation with the NCB and the Council the original has been placed in the Aber-Afon Council Archives but not before four copies were produced. The Council have one kept in the Council office, the NCB have one and we have one at our NUM office in the village. The fourth, it has been unanimously agreed, should go to you and your family, so I am pleased, in the presence of Mr Wright and Mr Collins to hand it to you now."

"I am deeply moved Max, and wish to thank you gentlemen very much." Stanford exclaimed. "It is a document of exceptional historic value but beyond that, a testimony to the true courage of Clive Harding and an account of the suffering of those tragic souls; it will be placed among the Stanford archives as a reminder that in former times they adhered to former standards that we are grateful we do not subscribe to today nor ever will."

Together they proceeded to the site. Forester first pointed to the stone wall as they walked beside it and commented on its quality.

"It was built by a firm of specialists in the art of stonewalling, of which there are few remaining. They have deliberately created an antiquated finish, in keeping with both the graveyard stone wall and the church itself; so that the whole effect is one of age, and I think, apart from those acquainted with period architecture, most of us would be of the impression that all these features are of the same origin."

They passed through the wooden gate, also a revival of an earlier design, and into the burial site. From here on in, the graves were lying to their right and left as they walked down the wide gravel pathway. Edward Stanford was impressed with the crossed shovel and mandrel depicted in the centre of each of the horizontal gravestones.

"That is a sentimental and significant touch, Max, and the complete uniformity of the whole layout is also an important feature; it encompasses the togetherness of the lost miners, united in an eternal bond."

When they came to the intersecting path, which led one way to the border with the field and the other to the lich-gate, they walked towards the field where near the wall stood a five foot monolith at the head of which was depicted a cob and dram and beneath was inscribed the following epitaph and the names of the twenty-five men and boys:

This monument was raised to commemorate the twenty-five

men and boys, appended below, who lost their lives and liberty

In the Pentrebach Level mining disaster of

January 1863.

By an act of pure serendipity they were discovered

and recovered in the year 1956.

This burial ground is, therefore, both their

sanctuary and their final resting place.

R. I. P.

Clive Harding	Deputy/shotsman
Evan Grffiths	Collier
Edward Jones	Deputy/shotsman
Wilfred Hallet	Collier
Samuel Thorn	Repairer
Byron Pike	Collier
Ivor Williams	'Alliar'
Edrid Francis	Collier
William Evans	'Alliar'
Shaun O'Grady	Collier
Thomas Bishop	Collier
Michael Donovan	Collier
Walter Jones	Collier
Jeremiah O'Conner	Collier
Sidney Llewellyn	Collier
Andrew Lloyd	Collier

George Thomas   Collier
Collin Morris   Collier

Edwin Rees   Collier
Kenneth Jones   Collier's assistant

Clifford Edwards Collier
Brian Jones   Collier's assistant

Bernard Bishop   Collier
Fredrick Lloyd   Collier's assistant
Hugh Lloyd   Collier's trainee

The commemorative monument kept the gathering in silence as each one of them absorbed its contents. It was Doctor Carmichael who spoke first when he addressed Forester.

"What has been achieved here is quite remarkable Mr Forester. I recall when you and I first engaged with one another and your response to my suggestion that the miners' remains be removed in secret and disposed of by the government. How offended you were by the words 'disposed of.' You soon made it plain that nothing was going to be done in secret and that the people of Pentrebach village should play at least a part in arranging the last resting place of those poor souls. I had been put in my place Mr Forester and today I am pleased to say; thank God for that."

Forester simply smiled and the party moved on towards the splendid oak lich-gate. After passing through into the graveyard, Forester asked if they would all turn round and view the gate from that side. In bold letters over the head of the lich-gate was inscribed the following:

They once were lost but now are found,

at last at peace beneath the ground.

Edward Stanford took Forester by the hand and shaking it vigorously declared:

"You've done them proud, Max. You've really done them proud."

And the small party, including Councillor Ben Collins, once his constant adversary, gathered round and applauded Max Forester, in an act of true gratitude and appreciation.

Printed in Great Britain
by Amazon